TRAVEL
ADVISORY

TRAVEL ADVISORY

STORIES OF MEXICO

David Lida

William Morrow and Company, Inc.

New York

It is the policy of William Morrow and Company, Inc., and its imprints and affiliates, recognizing the importance of preserving what has been written, to print the books we publish on acid-free paper, and we exert our best efforts to that end.

Library of Congress Cataloging-in-Publication Data
Lida, David.
Travel advisory : stories of Mexico / David Lida.—1st ed.
p. cm.
Contents: Bewitched—Free trade—Taxi—A beach day—La quedada—Regrets—Prenuptial agreement—The recruiting officer —Shuttered—Acapulco gold.
ISBN 0-688-17406-X (alk. paper)
1. Mexico—Social life and customs Fiction. 2. Americans—Travel—Mexico Fiction. I. Title.
PS3562.I325T7 2000
813'.54—dc21   99-23557
CIP

Printed in the United States of America

First Edition

1 2 3 4 5 6 7 8 9 10

Book design by Bernard Klein

www.williammorrow.com

Para Yehudit Mam, con pasión, locura y frenesí

Contents

Travel
Advisory

Bewitched

*W*hen Rhoda arrived at the Posada del Tigre it was already ninety degrees in Quetzalmaco and, typical of Gulf Coast towns in the summer, deeply, stultifyingly humid. The air in the lobby was still. The man behind the desk seemed to be asleep with his eyes open. Rhoda stepped around a skinny orange dog dozing heavily in the middle of the stone floor. It was ten-thirty in the morning.

She had come to Quetzalmaco to investigate magic, witchcraft, enchantment. But first she would have to attend to the prosaic. Arousing the blank-faced man from his stupor, she asked for a room.

Eusebio—manager, bellboy, and desk clerk in one—noted the straight blond bangs of her neck-length pageboy and her aquamarine eyes under gold-framed glasses. A *gringa*. "I have a room with air-conditioning," he said. Rhoda, after long experience traveling in Mexico, asked to see it before agreeing to spend the night.

Dutifully stepping from behind the desk, Eusebio, slender and short with copper-colored skin, a crown of leonine gray hair, and heavy-lidded eyes, gripped Rhoda's two suitcases. As he expected, they were heavy. Gringos owned many things and didn't like to leave them unattended while they traveled.

"*Pásele,*" he said, gesturing so she would walk ahead of him as he guided her outside the lobby and down the Posada's motor court. The bags might be cumbersome, but at least he could watch her stride before him, pleasantly scrutinizing her hips and buttocks, encased in roomy seersucker shorts, cinched by a white cotton belt.

He opened a forest green door and Rhoda regarded what she characterized as a standard hundred-peso Mexican hotel room: on the dark side, with a slightly dank odor of disinfectant. There were heavy green curtains, a cracked tile floor, and a phone and a TV that might actually work. In the bathroom there would be two flimsy towels and soap but no shampoo. She could stay in this room but wondered if she could do better within the hotel's confines.

"May I see one of the rooms upstairs with a view of the lake?" she asked. She spoke Spanish accurately, but like a child: slowly, precisely, one word at a time, with a gringo's untrilled *rs* and flat vowels. She had thin lips and an odd grimacing smile that seemed permanently engraved onto her face, revealing gleaming white dental work.

"*A sus órdenes,*" said Eusebio, grabbing her luggage and signaling for her to walk ahead. As they climbed the staircase, he watched her buttocks shift and imagined them as milky pink as Rhoda's face.

In Philadelphia, where Rhoda lived, men tended to eye her forty-two-year-old body with what they considered cold objectivity. They regarded her as over the hill, accustomed from TV commercials and magazine spreads to surgically enhanced prototypes half her age. She exercised habitually when at home, but was on the road much of the year, so couldn't keep up a perpetual schedule. Her skin had started to roughen and a network of tiny wrinkles had formed around her face. She noted with alarm that gravity had started to work on her neck, breasts, and buttocks. Her unpredictable diet on the road had widened her hips and thighs, and given her belly a convex shape. On the other hand, Eusebio found her adorable, if lamentably lean for a woman her age (which he figured at about thirty-five).

Each of the rooms upstairs had a little terrace with a metallic table, a white plastic chair, and a vista of the muddy freshwater lake that was one of Quetzalmaco's main attractions. Eusebio, one suitcase in each hand, urged her to the end of the hall, to show her one of the floor's largest rooms. But it had a stronger smell of disinfectant and peeling paint on the walls. Rhoda asked to see another.

"The others don't have air-conditioning," he warned. "They only have fans."

"*No problema,*" Rhoda assured him. "I prefer a fan." She didn't like to sleep with air-conditioning; its chill made her feel like a side of beef in a meat locker. She also knew the rooms with fans would be cheaper.

In the next room that Eusebio displayed, there was a tiny cluster of minuscule black ants crawling around the drain in the shower. Rhoda, concealing revulsion through her perpetual tight-mouthed smile, asked to see yet another. "Whatever you like," said Eusebio.

The next room was closer to her standards. Proudly, as if it were his own house, Eusebio showed her the terrace, the tiny bathroom with its shower the size of an upright coffin, the carafe filled with purified water on the bedside table. The rooms with air-conditioning, he explained, cost a hundred pesos, but he could let her have this one for eighty.

"I'll take it," she said.

"As you wish," he said, with a slight bow.

They went downstairs to the front desk so she could register. Before filling out the card, she said, in her deliberate, syllable-at-a-time Spanish, "I'm a journalist. I write travel articles about Mexico for newspapers in the United States. Do you have discount rates for journalists?"

Eusebio stared blankly at the large white teeth under her persistent smile. He didn't have an answer to her question, and in fact couldn't remember if a journalist had ever stayed at the hotel. "The price is already at a discount, *señorita*," he said, showing her a printed rate sheet. "We're allowed to charge one hundred and fifty pesos for the air-conditioned rooms and one hundred for the others; but since it's low season, we are happy to offer it to you for only eighty pesos."

"I understand," Rhoda said, her mouth tighter than ever. "But usually in Mexico I stay in hotels on a courtesy basis or at a large discount. My articles appear in thirty-eight newspapers in the United States and bring many tourists."

Eusebio was skeptical: nobody in Quetzalmaco read newspapers, and he doubted whether the gringos did either. Most of the tourists who passed through Quetzalmaco were *chilangos* anyway, from Mexico City. He knew that eighty pesos was a lot of money—he only earned forty a day. But he also knew that all gringos had money, even the young ones who carried backpacks, and wore torn jeans and sandals as if they were *campesinos*.

"Please," she said. "I know I can recommend this place to my readers."

There was something persuasive about the gringa. Eusebio wondered if she had powers. They wouldn't be the kind of powers some people had in Quetzalmaco—the witches, who could cure the sick with herbs, plants, and oils, or bring good luck or harm with spells. The gringos didn't go in for that. Eusebio had heard that their blood ran colder than the Mexicans', and that they didn't believe in God or the devil, only money.

"Let me see," he said. He was enchanted by her—the determined icy-blue eyes, the pink skin that had never lingered in the sun, her skinny buttocks. Besides, if he didn't budge, she'd just go around the corner to the Hotel Quetzalmaco. He sighed deeply. "Well, *señorita*," he said, "my boss will probably kill me. But I think I can let you have it for seventy pesos."

"Thank you so much," said Rhoda, the rigidity of her expression suddenly softening into a genuine smile. At the current exchange rate, she had just saved herself $1.30. The room would cost $9.

After checking in, Rhoda combed the hallway looking for a chambermaid. She found a brown girl in a pink smock, about sixteen, whose straight black hair was tied back with a rubber band. With excruciating slowness, she mopped the floor of the room next to Rhoda's. "*Buenos días*," said Rhoda.

The maid, thin in the upper body, but wide-hipped, ceased mopping. She said "*buen día*" to the blond foreigner but kept her eyes cast on the part of the floor she had just cleaned.

"What's your name?" asked Rhoda.

The maid looked up and considered the *gringa* suspiciously. "Yesenia," she said.

"I was wondering if you could do me a great favor," said Rhoda, slowly and deliberately. "I have a few clothes that I need washed— just some socks and T-shirts and underwear. Does the hotel have laundry service?"

After a brief pause the maid asked, "Did you ask them downstairs?"

"No, Yesenia," said Rhoda. "I haven't said anything to anyone but you."

Yesenia was silent. "Well, I could wash them for you, if you like," she finally said.

"Great," said Rhoda. "But I'm leaving tomorrow morning, so I need them today."

"I'll wash them right now," said Yesenia.

Rhoda collected her small pile of clothing in a plastic bag and brought it to the maid. "How much would it cost for you to do me this favor?" she asked.

Yesenia again cast her eyes to the floor. "Whatever you like, *señora*." She smiled.

Rhoda fished around in her change purse. "Would twenty pesos be all right, Yesenia?"

"*Sí, señora*," said the maid, eagerly collecting the coins. That was almost an entire day's minimum wage, and five pesos more than her cousin Eusebio paid her: the price of a couple of Coca-Colas, an ice cream, and a colorful barrette for her hair. "There's one thing, *señora*," she said awkwardly. "Since I am doing this for you, could you please not say anything to the people downstairs?" Cousin or no, Eusebio would fire her if he found out she was making any money on the side.

"My mouth is closed," said Rhoda. She pantomimed buttoning her lips together.

Yesenia looked at her quizzically. Was that some kind of secret sign? Yesenia's mother, who believed in witches' spells, was always making such strange gestures. "*Gracias, señora*," she said.

Rhoda knew she could trust the girl with her clothing because her job depended on it. She liked to go straight to the maids with her dirty laundry—not just because she paid them less than she would to the management, but in this manner the money went into the poor maid's, rather than the hotel owner's, pocket.

Rhoda walked back to her room and closed the door behind her. It was close to noon and broiling. She drew the curtains, opened the windows, and turned on the ceiling fan. Warily eyeing the carafe of water at the bedside, she opened her suitcase to remove one of what Eusebio had assumed were her precious possessions: a liter-and-a-half bottle of spring water she'd brought from Philadelphia. In Mexico, Rhoda only drank bottled water. In small towns in remote places she didn't necessarily trust the bottles, either; for occasions such as this, she carried her own.

She drank deeply, greedily, allowing a small trickle to drip down to her chin and dark blue T-shirt. Then she took the bottle outside to the little terrace, and sat in the heat, watching tiny ripples in the murky water of the lake. The area had been rain forest until the 1940s, when good roads were built and the land was cultivated. The town smelled of soil and sweet grasses, mangoes and wild-flowers. Suddenly there was a breeze. Rhoda closed her eyes and let it engulf her. In moments like these, after protracted negotiation, she loved Mexico.

Rhoda didn't believe in witches. In her imagination they elicited nothing more evocative than characters from the corniest television programs of her childhood: an effeminate ham with black bangs and an English accent on *Dark Shadows,* a pert housewife with a twitching nose on *Bewitched.*

She had observed with a mixture of curiosity and amusement that the Mexicans indeed gave credence to witchcraft. In every market in the country there seemed to be at least one stall selling mysterious multicolored candles, special oils and herbs, as well as boxes of soaps and packets of powders that promised, in words and pictures, good luck, success, protection for the home, or new hair growth. She thought of various friends who could have used a soap whose box depicted a woman with a gag over her mouth, and was marked *jabón de callarme:* soap to shut me up. Other packages had more enigmatic labeling: The Seven African Powers. The Panther's Leap. The Great Black Feather.

A few years earlier, while strolling through the Sonora Market in Mexico City, Rhoda, frustrated by a succession of cardboard suitors—restless married men and penitent premature ejaculators, creepy closet cases and dithering noncommitters—had considered buying a powder that conjured the love of a strong man. But at the last moment reason overtook impulse. Rhoda knew that the life that she'd chosen, in which nearly half her time was spent on the road, all but precluded serious involvement with anyone.

And she didn't mind. Most men, after fucking you once or twice with little expertise, acted as if they'd done you a great favor and immediately began to criticize your body, your clothing, your most ingrained habits. Who needed the bother? Who needed them at all? Her many travels were a superb sublimation for sex, and Rhoda had numerous friends in Philadelphia, mostly single women, histrionic gay men, and married couples with children (to whom she played the eccentric aunt, bearing exotic trinkets).

Today, however, with an assignment to interview a witch in Quetzalmaco, she understood another reason why she hadn't bought that powder in the Sonora Market: Mexican witchcraft frightened her. A little. Of course she knew it was nonsense—a mixture of superstition, old wives' tales, misplaced religious faith. The famous Quetzalmaco witches were notoriously phony, an attraction to lure tourists to a stifling swamp in the armpit of the Gulf Coast with few restaurants, bad weather, and scant tourist infrastructure.

Still, you never knew. It seemed safer to maintain a distance from such people and practices. Although she'd read an article in *National Geographic* that made nonspecific accusations that the

Quetzalmaco witches were "charlatans" and "blackmailers," it had also evoked cases where they'd reputedly killed with the use of toxic herbs, poisonous bat droppings, or slashing the jugular vein with extracted lions' teeth.

In any case, she had to relinquish her reticence—in the space of a few months, three editors had suggested a story about a visit with a Quetzalmaco witch. It was a good idea; she knew she'd be able to sell the article to a dozen more. Quetzalmaco was an inexpensive destination (Rhoda's specialty), off the beaten path but accessible, and of course witches were mysterious, sexy, even funny. At least from the perspective of a worldly American.

As she walked around the stifling, humid little town, she realized she would have no trouble finding a witch. Along the boardwalk by the lake, lined with banana palms with bulky drooping leaves, dozens of compact brown men stood, offering tours in motorboats. She refused them all, after which every third or fourth man asked, *Quiere brujo?* You want to see a witch? Some witches had even painted advertisements in bright colors on the town's walls: *Consejero en ciencias ocultas* and *Bótanico auténtico* and *Retiro maleficios*.

One ad stood out, for its enormity and verbosity. Atop a white-painted brick wall, scrawled in red letters, was the legend The Slithering Snake—The Power of Black. Underneath, in black and yellow and red, a man with an elaborate name that combined both Mexicos, before and after the conquest—Fulgencio Moctezuma Azcárraga—claimed he could take away illnesses difficult to cure, bring back lost lovers, deliver good luck in business, and remove spells, jinxes, and sexual impotence. Absolute Seriousness and Discretion Assured. Good enough, thought Rhoda. Let's get it over with.

Quetzalmaco was so small that his house, three blocks from the central plaza, was easy to find. It was on a quiet, residential street, naked and unprotected from the assault of the glaring sun. The denizens here were prosperous; their squarish, one-story modern homes, all with front porches, were made of brick and stone, metal and tile (rather than the flimsy wood and scavenged tin of poor neighborhoods). Everyone's front door remained open.

Including her witch's. The wall of his house had been painted with a similar advertisement to the one that had attracted her. Rhoda quietly stepped from the baking sidewalk to his porch, and looked inside the comfortably shady parlor. She saw no one, and gingerly stepped inside.

The furniture was nearly new, although unremarkable—a plump sky-blue sofa, a stuffed rocker, a glass-topped table surrounded by wooden chairs. Rhoda drifted to an arch in the wall, which led to an outdoor patio. There she noticed a black dog dozing in the shade of a fragrant orange tree, and a still, glum-faced piglet tethered to the wall. She had the sensation that they had been in the same position for a thousand years. A rooster bopped across the grass; it was so quiet that Rhoda could hear his footsteps.

"*Bienvenida,*" said a deep baritone voice. The surprise of it startled Rhoda so sharply that she felt her bowels tighten. As she turned around, her jaw involuntarily constricted and the stiff grimacing smile appeared on her face.

"*Buenas tardes,*" she said, slowly, deliberately, facing a man in the stuffed rocker. "You are Fulgencio Moctezuma Azcárraga?" Rhoda was absolutely confounded as to how he could have entered the room and seated himself without making a sound.

"*Sí, señorita,*" he answered. "In what manner can I serve you?" He had sleek black hair combed back from his forehead, and gleaming, toffee-colored skin. He wore a beige polyester shirt opened to the navel and several shiny gold chains across his chest. He also wore various gold rings, and when he spoke, revealed four front teeth capped in gold. His eyes were raven-colored, intense, and penetrating.

In fact, his gaze pierced Rhoda to the point of intimidation. She ignored the interior alarm, straightened her back and walked over to the man. "My name is Rhoda Coldwell," she said, handing him a business card. "I'm a journalist from the United States. I write about Mexico for thirty-eight newspapers all over the country."

The man stood up, revealing himself to be an inch or so shorter than Rhoda, but sturdy, thick, barrel-chested. He shook her hand gently. "It's a pleasure to meet you, *señorita,*" he said. "How I can help you?"

"I was hoping you'd let me interview you, Señor Moctezuma. I am sure that many readers in the United States would like to know about the witches in Quetzalmaco."

Moctezuma smiled, the gold in his mouth shining. He looked as if he was deciding whether he should talk to her or eat her. "Certainly," he said. "It would be a great pleasure for me. Please step into my chamber, where I do my work."

They passed through a black velvet curtain into a shadowy, low-ceilinged room, lit by bare bulbs of feeble wattage. The walls were painted black and covered with dusty snapshot photographs attached with thumb tacks. At one end of the room was a platform structure with tiered shelves, bearing candles striped in various colors, and large plastic bottles of tinted liquids—blue, yellow, green, red. Atop the platform were a few scattered figures—a devil, an owl, a serpent, a black panther.

Moctezuma stood to one side of a table laid with a black satin cloth, atop which were dozens of little plastic bags, containing miniature horseshoes and packets bearing the image of Saint Martin on horseback, which Rhoda recognized as a traditional Mexican symbol of good luck.

"Sit down," said Moctezuma, taking a chair on one side of the table. He stared at her fixedly. "I have been a witch for thirty-two years," he said.

Rhoda's smile was in place, as were the pen and notebook she had fished out of her handbag. "You started out as a child?" she asked.

"I was nineteen," said Moctezuma. "I am fifty-one years old."

"You look much younger than that," said Rhoda, hoping to score points with her compliment.

Moctezuma ignored her remark and continued, his eyes unswerving from her face. "My father, Fernando Moctezuma, died at the age of seventy-nine. He was a witch for forty-six years." Rhoda nodded, smiling. "Write that down," he said. Rhoda obeyed.

"My uncle, Raimundo Moctezuma, died at the age of ninety-two. He was a witch for seventy-seven years. My grandmother, Gumara Gracia, lived to be one hundred and seventeen. She was a witch for ninety-nine years." His expression had assumed a frightening gravity. "*Write that down,*" he said sharply. There was a vague physical threat, as if he'd smother her if she didn't. "Her uncle, Piedad Lozano Mayor, died at eighty-six years. . . ."

Soon Rhoda became dizzy with all the numbers, ages, dates. She got the point—he claimed to come from a long line of witches. Was he trying to lull her into a hypnotic state? She emitted a light sigh.

The relaxed smile had returned to Moctezuma's face. "You are bored with all this information about my family?" he asked.

"No, no, not at all," stammered Rhoda, returning his smile with her tighter one, "it's just that I won't have space to include . . ."

"*Está bien,*" said Moctezuma agreeably. "Permit me to tell you more about what I do." He paused dramatically. "I am a specialist in black magic," he said. "Do you know what *la maldad negra* is?"

Rhoda, feverishly taking notes, wondered how she'd translate this phrase—the black evil? "Not really," she said.

"All illness, all accidents, all bad luck, and even death are caused by *la maldad negra*," said Moctezuma. "I can take away *la maldad negra* by bringing in *el poder blanco*," he continued. White power—Rhoda wondered if any African-Americans would write angry letters to the editor after reading the article. "*El poder blanco* overtakes *la maldad negra*," continued the witch. "With white prayer, I can unearth what has been buried in the graveyard by black prayer; the white cures the black."

Luckily, he spoke slowly, so Rhoda could follow nearly every word, and keep scribbling notes. "What kind of people come to see you?" she asked.

"Primarily very sick people, who have been disillusioned by doctors. If someone has cast a spell on you, you cannot be cured by a traditional doctor with pills or syrups—you need to see a witch. I have cured people of cancer. I have helped the lame to walk. Once a man who had been bewitched came to me. His tongue was hanging out of his mouth—it was enormous and dripping, like the tongue of a dog. I cured him, too."

This was patently ridiculous, thought Rhoda. "How did you do it?" she asked.

Moctezuma, staring in her eyes, said, "I invoked God and the Great Lord of the Fog."

"Who is that?" she asked.

"Lucifer." His eyes seemed to change from black to gray. It was spooky, but Rhoda was on to him: he had moved his head slightly and thus the shifting light changed them.

"How do you, um, evoke them?" asked Rhoda.

Suddenly his eyes, rolling back in his head, turned to white, and he appeared to be in a trancelike state. "O sirs," he incanted in a strangely high-pitched voice, "please come to me, favorably and amiably under my orders. God, go near Satan and put him in the light." Just as suddenly Moctezuma snapped out of it, his eyes in place, smiling through his gold teeth. "Satan obeys the light, you see."

The room was sticky and musty. Rhoda felt an uncomfortable surge of blood through her body; her nipples stiffened. She ignored this reaction. "So you're a good witch," she said, writing. "When you say you specialize in black magic, you mean you overtake 'the power of black' with 'the power of white'?"

Rhoda found his eyes at her breasts, which were small and, at least when supported by an underwire bra, sociably pert. "I can also call forth *la maldad negra,* and cause great harm, even death," he said. "All I need is someone's name, an article of their clothing, and their photograph."

Rhoda looked at the plethora of snapshots on the wall. She focused on one, a black-and-white portrait of a smiling man wearing a slender tie, horn-rimmed glasses and a nerd's crew cut. It looked like a college yearbook photo from 1965. And then another, newer, in color, of a curly-haired fat woman in a floral housecoat. Rhoda gestured toward the wall. "You mean, all of these—"

"Yes," said Moctezuma before she could complete her sentence. From under the table, he produced an object wrapped in stained newspaper. He unwrapped it and showed Rhoda a doll fashioned from what looked like parachute silk, dyed dark brown and tied in place with black thread. It gave her the heebie-jeebies.

"Is that stained with coffee?" asked Rhoda.

"Touch it," said Moctezuma, his eyes more forceful and sinister than ever. Under her fingers, the doll was slippery, greasy. "That's not coffee," he said. "It's the oil of the dead."

Rhoda felt another strange tingling in her body. Now she understood why people vaguely accused the witches of intimidation, blackmail, trickery. They make you think they have the power to kill, and then persuade you to pay them not to use that power against you.

"Let me ask you another question," she said. She spoke more slowly than ever; the query was difficult in Spanish. "When someone hires you to harm someone else, do you ever suspect that the person you're bewitching hasn't done anything bad? And that the bad guy is the one who's hiring you?"

Moctezuma nodded.

"Doesn't that make you feel guilty? That you're harming someone who is innocent?"

The witch furrowed his brow, as if her question was so esoteric that it had never occurred to him. Then he shrugged. "If someone pays me," he said, "I have to perform. Otherwise, they say that I'm a liar, that I have no powers."

Rhoda nodded. *Typical Mex lack of morality,* she scrawled in her notebook. A droplet of sweat fell from her chin to the page. "Thank God, I am in very good health at the moment," she said, tapping Moctezuma's table with her knuckles, assuming that under the velvet cloth it was made of wood. "And I can't think of anyone in particular who I want to cast a spell on. So I'm trying to think, why would I come to you? If I wanted to be a client?"

The witch nodded, and immediately asked, "You're not married, are you?"

How did he know? When she traveled Rhoda always wore a gold band on the appropriate finger to deflect such conjectures. "No," she admitted.

He leaned back and stared at her with his probing eyes. Rhoda felt that not only could he see her naked body but also her blood, bones, entrails. "There is a man, but he has been frustrated in his intention to enchant you," he said.

Sure, she thought. She decided once again that the witch was a complete charlatan. "I don't think so," she said quickly, with a short, dismissive laugh. "Not really."

"Oh, yes, there is," said Moctezuma. "I am certain he is there. He has dark hair, and he's a little older than you. You haven't yet sensed him because you are suffering from a *maldad,* from *envidias.*"

Envidias . . . jealousies. Well, sure, thought Rhoda. Who isn't prone to envy? The names of a couple of travel writers whose bylines she saw more frequently than her own crossed her mind, the no-talents who got the big-money assignments in *Travel & Leisure* and *Town & Country*. But what did that have to do with the man with dark hair?

"You have been unlucky in love because there are people who are jealous of you," said Moctezuma, with assurance so unwavering that it seemed almost tyrannical. "They have put spells on you to prevent you from finding this man."

Rhoda sighed. If only it were that simple. A movie featuring all the pallid, obnoxious, or unattainable men she'd met in the last couple of years ran in her mind. She was developing a sort of wry respect for Moctezuma. He knew how to find a weak spot and then play it like a violin.

"If you wish, I can give you a *limpia,*" said Moctezuma. "I can cleanse you of the *maldad,* so you can find your man."

"Okay," said Rhoda cheerfully. What the hell. It would add a lot of color to her article.

"Move to this chair, please," said Moctezuma, indicating an old wooden seat in the middle of the room. "Repeat after me."

Moctezuma began to incant a prayer. "Oh, Lord, send me San Pedro," he said. "Send me San Martín the Horseman. And Santa

Elena. And San Guillermo of the Glass of Red Wine." Rhoda felt
like a complete idiot repeating these words, but nonetheless ech-
oed Moctezuma with enthusiasm because she didn't want to insult
him. After all, what if he was real? What if he *could* find her a man?

"Send me these saints, oh, Lord, and send me Lucifer, Satan,
the devil—the Great Lord of the Fog. Send your knights forth to
bring him out of the mist into the light." As Rhoda repeated, the
witch picked up one of the bottles from the altar, which contained
a brackish green liquid.

"Take off your glasses," he said. She obeyed, placing them on
the altar. Chanting, he poured some of the sticky green fluid onto
his hand and rubbed it on her face, then some more on her neck.
And then he upended a half pint over her head.

The dousing didn't come as a complete surprise—Rhoda had
read in *National Geographic* that it was a part of many witches'
ceremonies. But the slimy texture and the smell, a bracing mixture
of herbs and alcohol, were shocking. She kept on mimicking his
words as if unfazed.

"Take away *la maldad negra* from your obedient daughter—all
illness, all harm, all frights," he said. He poured more of the liquid
on her exposed arms, atop her shoulders and breasts and lap, and
with his hands spread it around her knees. He pulled off her sandals
and dripped it on her naked feet. It didn't seem to stain, but Rhoda
wondered what she'd smell like on the walk back to her hotel.

"Especially take away the spell that has caused her sentimental
and emotional problems, her obstacles to love. Save her from the
enchanted snakes that have been buried in the black graveyard.
Basil, rosemary, and rue, bring her salvation and good luck."

Moctezuma grabbed a bottle of blue liquid, filled his mouth
with it until his cheeks bulged, and then spit its contents over her
head in a warm, sputtering stream. Rhoda was getting the hang of

the *limpia;* the shower felt oddly pleasurable. Best of all, she knew she had good copy, the stuff of a salable article. He repeated the spitting process twice, and then grabbed from atop the altar the small branch of a tree, thick with smooth circular leaves of pale green. He handed Rhoda the bottle with the blue liquid, and held the branch before her. "Wet it," he said.

"The leaves?" she asked.

"Wet it!" She poured, and he turned the branch over. "Wet it!" he commanded again. She covered the other side.

Now Moctezuma was rapidly chanting words that Rhoda couldn't understand, let alone repeat. They weren't Spanish, but Indian, from one of the Gulf Coast's indigenous languages. He began to rub the wet leaves all over her head, neck, and torso. Then he got on his knees, and gestured that she do the same.

It was strange, and silly, but even though she could barely see, her glasses on the altar, the colored liquids stinging her eyes, Rhoda felt somehow safe, even comfortable, in this bizarre encounter. The witch rubbed his branch around her arms and torso and waist, and finally under her T-shirt.

She was reassured by the fact that Mexicans had been performing this nonsense for centuries; Moctezuma, in some crazy way, must truly believe in his powers. She felt sorry, and poignantly sad, that she couldn't believe as well. For a long time, her joy of discovery and adventure had offset her lack of belief, but two decades of travel for a living had erased most of those feelings, too.

But she felt *something* as Moctezuma rubbed the leaves along her chest under her T-shirt, and her perspiration commingled with the herbs and the alcohol, and the front clasp of her bra unsnapped. Something she hadn't felt in a long time, a pagan thrill that reminded her of the promise of dirty encounters in her high school days, encounters that never quite came off. She let out a short, husky laugh.

Still babbling in his indigenous tongue, Moctezuma, with gentle pressure on Rhoda's back, guided her toward the ground until she was on all fours. He rubbed the leaves around the back of her head and neck, and across the narrow frame of her back from her shoulders to her tailbone. Then he rubbed her stretched buttocks across the thin cotton of her seersucker shorts. He was practically shouting his incantation as he began to lunge the leafy branch back and forth between her legs.

Blood flushed her face red. Rhoda hadn't had sex in a year; sex with anyone she'd particularly liked, or uninhibited sex with abandon, in several years; and sex outside of a bed since she was in college. She'd certainly never in her life had sex with the lubricated and leafy branch of a tree brandished by a Mexican witch. Something else she'd never had, except when induced by her own hands, was an orgasm, and she felt so sensationally close to one now that she stopped breathing.

And then another Rhoda materialized, a Rhoda not squatting like a dog but standing upright, a yard away at Moctezuma's desk. This Rhoda, gazing at the spectacle in which her counterpart was participating, shook her head reproachfully.

"Hey!" shouted the Rhoda on the floor, and grabbed at the branch, tugging it out of Moctezuma's grasp. She swung it in the air in front of him as she clumsily propelled herself upright, and grabbed at her eyeglasses. "That's about enough, pal," she said in English, the tight smile stretched across her flossed and shiny teeth, her breath rapidly expanding her chest. As she grasped her purse, she held the branch in front of her like a weapon.

On the ground, his shiny black hair spilling across his forehead, his shirt released from the waistband of his pants, Moctezuma's frame was a disorderly blend of amber skin and pastel fabric, sweat and radiant gold. "*Señorita*," he announced through labored breaths, "you are cured."

"Yeah, I'll bet," said Rhoda. Without waiting for Moctezuma, she pushed the velvet curtain aside and walked into his bright parlor. She almost continued out the door, but stopped short.

If he was real, he could harm her. She didn't want to offend him so much that he would. She worried that perhaps she already had. He had her card, with her name and address. She decided to wait and politely say good-bye.

She turned toward the patio to reach under her T-shirt and clasp her bra, and then glanced outside. The black dog snored lightly, and the rooster pecked at the ground. The moody piglet, still tethered to the wall, snorted. She wondered if the menagerie played a part in Moctezuma's witchcraft. She had read something in *National Geographic* about animal transferences, or people's manifestations as animals, or something like that.

She heard a click and quickly looked up. Moctezuma, appearing from his chamber, had just snapped her picture with a cheap point-and-shoot camera. His hair impeccably combed, his beige shirt newly tucked, his gold mouth twinkling, as fresh as when she'd first seen him.

"Is the pig used for *brujería*?" Rhoda asked, stammering and blushing.

"Excuse me?" asked Moctezuma.

"The pig," she insisted. "Do you use it for witchcraft?"

"No." He smiled. "I'm going to fatten him up and eat him."

Rhoda wondered if she should ask him about paying a fee—but no. That would be giving him money to stop him from hurting her; she wouldn't participate in the blackmail of the Quetzalmaco witches. "Thank you very much, *señor*," she said, and stretched her arm stiffly before her to shake his hand.

He placed a little plastic bag with the horseshoe and Saint Martin in her palm. "This is for luck," he said. In his hand was also a fat stack of business cards held together with a rubber band. "For your American acquaintances."

She looked at the top card. It said much the same as the signs on the walls: The Slithering Snake—The Power of Black. There was an illustration of a gracefully curving black snake. "It really was . . . an experience," said Rhoda, smiling tensely. "I'll send you a copy of the article when it's published." She knew she wouldn't.

Moctezuma smiled painfully. She marched outside.

Rhoda shampooed his green and blue fluids out of her hair, and scrubbed them off her body. She combed the hotel looking for Yesenia the chambermaid, to wash her T-shirt and seersucker shorts, and even her bra and panties, which were imbued with the herbal-alcohol scent of the witch's solutions. Yet despite these efforts, she was unable to erase Moctezuma from her mind's eye.

After dark, ravenous with hunger, she sat at a wooden table in the corner of a restaurant's outdoor patio, overlooking a jungly overgrowth. The murkiness of the foliage at night, the shrill chirping of the crickets, the penetrating dark eyes and pulsating throat of an iguana in a mango tree, lit by a fixture on the restaurant's ceiling, were all sinister reminders of the witch's presence a few streets away. "*Mamá! Papá!*" suddenly squawked a parrot from inside the kitchen. Rhoda was so startled she practically jumped from her seat.

She was sure that food would calm her down. In the excitement of the afternoon she had completely forgotten to eat lunch. Impatiently, she watched a stocky young waiter scuttle around a long table where a large, prosperous-looking group of gabbing adults and screeching children was eating. Rhoda couldn't hear what they were saying, but she noted with agony that everyone seemed to have a special request for the waiter.

Finally he approached her table. He was perspiring heavily, wearing a black vest over his white shirt despite the heat in the patio, where a slow-moving ceiling fan did absolutely nothing to move the stagnant air. Rhoda impulsively decided to order a cocktail, something she rarely did—but she needed to wipe out the stress of her earlier encounter. Before she could open her mouth, however, the waiter said, "I'll be with you *ahorita*," and sped off to clear the plates from another table.

Ahorita. She let out a long sigh—she wanted that drink. *Ahorita* was a diminutive form of the word *ahora,* which means *now.* That the Mexicans trifled with the word *now* meant they had a familiar and flexible relationship with its meaning, and unburdened them of its responsibility. She sighed again, tensely: *ahorita* could mean five minutes, or forty-five minutes, or six weeks. The parrot unexpectedly squawked from the kitchen again: "*Mamá! Papá!*" Rhoda shuddered.

When the waiter returned—this time bearing a shrimp cocktail, asking which member of the large group had ordered it, despite the fact that they were all eating their main courses—Rhoda waved at him. He held up a hand with his thumb and forefinger pressed together, a visual manifestation of *ahorita.*

The waiter managed to palm off the shrimp cocktail on one of the diners. Rhoda again waved at the waiter, but he disappeared into the kitchen.

Along with the hunger, in the pit of her stomach she began to feel a wave of despondency. She had been traveling in Mexico for more than fifteen years, and had at first enjoyed incredible experiences. But the excitement was hardly exponential. At this stage in her life she was no longer comfortable, let alone happily disposed, to clomp from town to town in second-class buses, sleep in clammy hotel rooms, suffer such inept service. Not to mention undergo embarrassing, disturbing encounters with witches.

Finally the waiter came to her table, breathing heavily. Her eyes bore in on his through the gold-framed glasses. Her smile was clamped in place. "Please," she said, in her deliberate manner. "I'm incredibly thirsty. Could you bring me a rum and a mineral water, as soon as possible?"

"*Sí, señorita,*" said the waiter. "Excuse me . . ." He pointed to the crowded patio, explaining his inattention.

How long would it take? She sighed again, staring at the tangled overgrowth, smelling muskily of soil. To her pleasant surprise, he returned briskly, with a fizzing cocktail, in a tall glass with ice, a white straw poking above the surface. Alongside was a small dish of fragrant sections of lime, which he'd sliced with his own hands.

"No, no, no, no, no." Rhoda smiled. "*Primero.* Is the ice in this drink from purified water?"

The waiter quickly looked at his other tables. "Yes, of course, *señorita,*" he said quickly.

The waiter was probably telling the truth, but Rhoda wouldn't be so easily dismissed. She had to establish that she knew what she was talking about, and wasn't just another stupid *gringa* easily taken advantage of.

"*Segundo.* I can't drink this," she announced through her riveted smile, handing him back the drink. "Please bring me the rum in a glass with ice. I want the mineral water on the side, but bring the bottle and open it here. I won't drink it if I can't see you open the bottle."

"*Como usted quiera,*" said the waiter.

"*Mamá! Papá!*" cried the bird from the kitchen.

Rhoda was satisfied she would now get what she wanted, but victories in Mexico were always bittersweet. As a consequence of her rebuke, he would take ages to bring her back the cocktail.

Rhoda's dejection began to tilt toward anger. Was it any wonder that Mexico suffered from so much crime, corruption, poverty? The people were impossible. At the big table, one of the couples was arguing, an older lady tried to quiet them, and the children ran around playing tag. They were just *backward*. She thought of Eusebio the lethargic hotel clerk, Yesenia the witless chambermaid (who hadn't yet brought back Rhoda's clothes), the inept waiter. And again the witch.

She became infuriated with the return of Moctezuma to her mind's eye, after a couple of minutes of successfully eluding his memory: his black hair, the glistening gold in his mouth and on his fingers and chest, and worst of all, his threatening gaze. He probably thought it was a big joke to humiliate her, to have an American woman on all fours in front of him. Some people were just warped.

Ultimately, the waiter brought the rum, carefully placed the bottle of mineral water in front of her, opened it, and poured for her. As she took her first long sublime draught, he smiled and bowed, and was about to go to another table, but she grabbed his forearm so forcefully that her nails almost broke his skin. "I'm ready to order," she said.

As an appetizer, she asked for *tegogolos*—a local word, probably Indian, for snails from the lake. According to her guidebook they were one of Quetzalmaco's specialties.

Snails. As she sipped her drink, she imagined the fat ones you get in Paris bistros, pried loose from their round shells and swimming in garlic butter. She could smell them, and even hear the strains of an accordion. Although ravenous, she didn't eat any of the steaming tortillas the waiter had brought in a basket. She wanted to postpone her pleasure until the snails arrived. Meanwhile, the rum drink both relaxed her and cooled her off on the steaming patio.

It took nearly a half hour, but her appetizer finally arrived. It was like nothing she'd ever seen before: an enormous plate of fat disks, like swollen checkers of orange and gray, no shells in sight.

They were cold, swimming in lemon juice, sliced onions, chopped tomatoes, and chile peppers. A snail ceviche. A frigid mollusk salad. Her guidebook hadn't mentioned this preparation. With a moue, she put one in her mouth. Briny, lemony, firecracker peppery, it had the texture of a rubber shower shoe, and it disgusted her.

Rhoda spit out the snail over the patio's banister into the overgrowth. They were trying to take advantage of her, just as that crooked gold-toothed bastard Moctezuma had. For the moment she entertained the panicky suspicion that the witch had cast a spell on her so she'd be poisoned in the restaurant.

She dropped her fork atop her plate; it clanked loudly. "Young man!" she called to the waiter, in a voice so loud that the rest of the customers looked at her.

He was adding the check at another table, and gave her that two-fingered *ahorita* signal. "Young man, please come here *now!*" she cried. She didn't care: let them look, like a stupid herd of cows. Her smile was more severe than ever.

The waiter shrugged apologetically at the people whose bill he was adding. They nodded understandingly. He trotted to Rhoda. "*Sí, señorita,* everything in order?" he asked.

"No, it certainly isn't," she said quickly. "These aren't snails."

He didn't understand. "I beg your pardon?"

"These aren't snails. I don't know what they are, but they aren't snails."

"They're *tegogolos,*" said the waiter uncomprehendingly. "Fresh from the lake this morning."

"These *things* are terrible. They taste like rubber bands in vinegar. This isn't the way that snails are supposed to be served."

She looked like she was going to kill someone. "But *señorita,*" said the waiter, "that's the way we've always served them in Quetzalmaco."

"Well then, you've always done it wrong!" said Rhoda, her eyes burning holes in the waiter, as Moctezuma's had in her. "Can't you ever admit that you're wrong? *I know how snails are supposed to be cooked!* And you just don't know how to cook snails!"

She screamed at the waiter as if possessed by a demon. "If you like," he said fearfully, "I can serve you something else instead."

"Yes, of course I want something else!" said Rhoda in a sharp breath. The situation seemed to calm imperceptibly. Some of the Mexican customers, who had been watching intently, laughed nervously or coughed into their napkins.

Again, the bird squawked, *"Mamá! Papá!"* Rhoda suddenly felt so utterly alone and unprotected that she began to cry convulsively, her elbows on the table, her face in her hands, her shoulders shaking. She hated Mexico. She hated travel.

Back at the hotel, Rhoda took a melatonin pill, and then another shower before she went to bed. She hoped that the steaming hot water would untie the knots of tension in her back. It had been one of those days that made her despair of her profession. After nearly twenty years of travel writing, she had to hustle to make ends meet, much more than when she'd started. Newspapers were flopping, folding, withering on the vine, and the cost-cutting management teams of the survivors were buying fewer freelance articles. Still, it beat a nine to five, she said to herself, the same mantra she'd been repeating all these years on the bad days.

She'd write an amusing article full of vivid description, but without specifically recommending Quetzalmaco as a tourist destination. The town was a bleak, sweltering, swampy backwater. The witches were frauds. Any Americans who came here would leave feeling they'd wasted their money.

Rhoda had finally got what she'd wanted in the restaurant (a shrimp cocktail and a tasty filet of red snapper in herb sauce, lubricated with two more soothing rum drinks). After her little tan-trum, the Mexicans had stopped staring at her, showing her the respect she deserved. The waiter attended her as if she were a visiting dignitary, even a queen. Which is how she thought she *should* have been treated. If the Mexicans wanted to attract foreign tourists, didn't they need to offer an international standard of service?

Finely fed, enjoying the scalding shower, she thought of her travails of the day. She could laugh now, about Eusebio, Yesenia, the waiter, and even Moctezuma. Rhoda reflected that traveling in Mexico was like baby-sitting a thousand infant children. The moment you detain one from painting a mural with your pancake makeup, she pondered with amusement, you turn and find another one hanging out the window. You grab him, set him in his crib, and spot a third shitting his diapers and a fourth powdering the kitchen with all-purpose flour. Containing the disaster was a full-time job.

When she opened her bag to separate the clothes she was going to wear the following day, her irritation briefly returned: she re-alized that Yesenia had not yet returned her dirty laundry. Well, if the chambermaid acted like an infant, at least she had an ex-cuse—she actually was an unschooled teenager. No matter; Rhoda would find her in the morning.

It was a delicious sensation—lying in bed, naked under the thin blanket, the ceiling fan cooling her pleasantly. She was so ex-hausted that she worried about being overtired and unable to sleep. Hence the melatonin pill, which guaranteed slumber, albeit of a strange sort, in which she'd wake up several times during the night, and then roll over and nod off again. She'd probably have odd, vivid dreams, which she'd forget as soon as she awoke.

As she began to drift into sleep, a dozen round, hard-backed beetles emerged from her shower's drain, marching in trooplike fashion into her room. Several lime green lizards silently found their way through the open window from a tear in the screen. A swarm of ants began to scatter in all directions from a hole in the light fixture and the cracks in the tiles. A couple of fat river rats, their whiskers twitching, appeared from under the dresser. A gleaming black snake crawled inside from a crack at the bottom of the door. Had Rhoda awakened and noticed the intrusion, she would have panicked, screaming in terror, unsure if what she saw was a dream.

FREE TRADE

i wonder what's keeping María Concepción," said Carmela Zorrilla, seated at her dining table. She glanced from her husband, Raimundo, folding his napkin in his lap, to her son, Félix, absently rubbing his newly grown mustache. Neither responded to her comment, and she felt the quiet keenly. Raimundo had never been much of a talker, and after their daughter, Adriana, married and left home a year earlier, Carmela realized how the two women had always dominated the conversation at meals. Félix, scowling slightly, seemed preoccupied of late. Carmela had no idea why.

There wasn't even the distraction of food in front of them, and the attendant clinking of china, silver, and crystal to subvert the stillness. The dining room faced the garden in back of their house in the Lomas section of Mexico City; the Zorrillas were so noiseless that Carmela could hear birds chirping outside.

"She's been as slow as a donkey lately," said Félix finally.

Raimundo, his thinning gray hair combed back, dressed in a white shirt and multicolored necktie, brushed invisible crumbs from his ample belly, and then checked his watch. It was almost three o'clock; he had to be back at the office by four-thirty or five at the latest. He enjoyed coming home to eat, but at this pace he'd surely be tardy.

Finally María Concepción entered, bearing a tray with three steaming bowls of chicken consommé. With conspicuous slowness, the nut-colored woman walked to the table and set one in front of each Zorrilla. Raimundo and Carmela thanked her as they received their soup; Félix snorted. María Concepción only nodded, and listlessly stepped back to the kitchen.

Raimundo immediately began to eat—slurping, to Carmela's dismay. The soup was delectable, as usual. His brown eyes, over their heavy bags, moved around the table.

"And the tortillas?" he asked his wife.

"María Concepción!" called Carmela. There was no answer. Carmela cleared her throat, and called for the maid again.

"*Sí, señora,*" María Concepción said, opening the kitchen door and taking one step in the room.

"The tortillas, please," said Carmela sternly.

"*Ay, sí,*" said María Concepción. Running a hand through her unevenly cut black hair, she popped back into the kitchen. She returned at once, carrying a basket of hot tortillas wrapped in a clean dish towel. She moved awkwardly, her backless slippers flapping. Her creased blouse hung unevenly outside of her baggy skirt. "*Gracias,*" said Raimundo, who watched her retreat to the kitchen. She appeared dumpier, and more unkempt, than usual.

María Concepción's tortillas, made by hand, were always luscious. He eagerly removed one from the basket, his eyes darting around the table again. "And the salsa?" he asked his wife.

Carmela let a sigh escape. "María Concepción," she called, her voice just short of a scream. "Would you please bring the salsa to the table?"

"*Pendeja,*" muttered Félix.

"Son!" said Raimundo, with some heat. "Apologize to your mother immediately."

"Sorry, Mamá," he said sourly. "But she's been acting like an imbecile lately."

Raimundo looked at his son with contempt. "The soup is excellent," he said pointedly.

"It needs salt," said Félix, shaking an enormous quantity into his bowl. "I think you should get rid of her, Mamá."

"Listen," said Raimundo, bristling. "When you become a housewife, it'll be your job to make such decisions. Until then, the *muchacha* is your mother's business."

Before Félix could retort, María Concepción clomped back into the room, holding a bowl of piquant green sauce, the condiment with which the Zorrillas peppered their food at every meal. "Excuse me," she said, smiling and thus exposing her cracked front tooth. "I don't know where my head is today." She giggled weakly and went back to the kitchen.

Carmela couldn't deny that María Concepción had been behaving oddly. Something was the matter, but what? It seemed to Carmela there was a congenital disease among *muchachas:* they worked industriously for a few years, and then a mysterious crisis occurred, and all the trust so painstakingly built fell to pieces in an instant.

María Concepción had come to work for the Zorrillas six years earlier, at the age of nineteen, just off the bus from a one-donkey town in the mountains of Oaxaca. She'd been recommended by her cousin Eugenia, the *muchacha* of the Parras, friends and neighbors of the Zorrillas.

María Concepción had proven to be such a dependable *muchacha* that Carmela wouldn't let her go without a fight. The house was always spotless. Carmela had exactingly taught her how much starch Raimundo liked in his shirts, how to take precise phone messages, and how to prepare all of the family's favorite dishes.

Even more importantly, María Concepción could be trusted. The Zorrillas could leave her alone in the house when they took vacations, in contrast to many of Carmela's friends, who complained that when they went away the *muchachas* stole things, raided the liquor cabinet, or tried on the *señora*'s clothes.

Nor did María Concepción ever complain about her 1,200-peso-per-month salary. The amount was the equivalent of $150, but it struck Carmela as reasonable, even generous: in their fair country, the minimum wage was only a little more than $3 a day. María Concepción also received free board, as well as her own eight-by-eight room behind the kitchen. The Zorrillas, considerately in Carmela's estimation, gave María Concepción a week's vacation every year so she could visit her daughter, and even threw in the bus fare to Oaxaca and a few extra pesos so she could bring some presents.

The maid had Sundays off and never seemed to need extra free time for "emergencies." Only once in a while did she ask for help with financial crises, usually involving medical or dental work for her daughter. After a series of exacting questions—Carmela didn't want the *muchacha* to think she was easily taken advantage of—she usually gave María Concepción the money.

Carmela watched María Concepción, who looked drawn and haggard, clear the soup bowls and pad back to the kitchen in her loose and shapeless clothes. Suddenly she realized the precise nature of her maid's problem.

Carmela held her tongue, though, as María Concepción sluggishly served the rice with carrots and *chayote,* then the pork loin *en adobo* and the refried beans, and finally the three-milk cake and coffee. "I was thinking about going to Polanco to get a good

Talavera platter as a wedding present for the Gutiérrez girl on Sunday," Carmela said to her husband.

"Whatever you like, darling," Raimundo said vacantly.

"Your blue suit is pressed, isn't it, Félix?" she asked.

"I guess so." Félix, slender and sullen, ran a hand through his receding hair, slicked back with mousse.

"You know Laura will be there, too," said Carmela. She referred to the younger, still unmarried, daughter of the Gutiérrez family. Félix didn't even bother to grunt. My *pobrecito,* thought Carmela. Twenty-eight years old, and still as glum and moody as a teenager. Her poor darling would iron out all his problems when he got married, in due time.

After the two men returned to work, Carmela lit a cigarette and went into the kitchen, where María Concepción washed the dishes.

Carmela sat in a chair. "How are things going, María Concepción?" she asked cheerfully.

"Everything's good, *señora,*" said the maid, her eyes on the soapy crockery.

"Are you sure?" asked Carmela. "Lately, you seem a little . . . distracted."

Although her head stayed in place, the *muchacha*'s eyes moved from the sink to the *señora* and then back again. She said nothing.

"María Concepción, may I ask you a question?"

"*Sí, señora,*" she said.

Carmela inhaled her cigarette, and asked, "Are you pregnant?" María Concepción stood there, still as a statue, the water running, the foamy sponge in her hand, her eyes on the dishes. She was frozen, immobile—what was the matter with her? And Carmela suddenly realized the *muchacha* was crying—mute and motionless, but weeping, with fat, salty tears spilling down her cheeks.

"Do you know who the father is?" Carmela asked. María Concepción said nothing and continued to cry. "Don't worry," Carmela said with a sigh. "Let's see what we can do."

María Concepción had been given drugs that made her woozy and confused, but when the contractions came, every five minutes or so, she felt a wrenching sensation of pain more intense than she could remember in her entire life. Was it possible that it hurt even more than the first time? She'd only been fifteen then; it *must* have been worse. On TV, she'd once heard someone say that people remember pleasure, but block out their memories of pain.

Suddenly she felt an appalling assault around her entire midsection, as if she were being ripped apart from the outside. She imagined torrents of blood gushing from her belly and between her legs, and gasped.

"Push," said the doctor, who had blue eyes and wore a green face mask. She could barely make him out—the overhead light was bright, sweat dripped from her forehead into her eyes, and the drugs clouded her vision.

It was true about pleasure and pain. María Concepción could vividly recall sitting in the park with her cousin Eugenia on a Sunday afternoon, sharing a Coca-Cola; or the first time she'd taken the bus from San Fermín el Chico to Mexico City (she'd had a window seat, and seen mountains, desert, and jungle); or those quiet, breezy afternoons when she stole a spare hour, sitting on the roof waiting for the Zorrillas' clothes, which she washed by hand, to dry. In contrast, she had only vague recollections of her father beating her, sometimes with his bare palms and sometimes with a switch he'd pulled from a tree; and that her uncle, her mother's own brother, had been even rougher, raping her repeatedly until she got pregnant and he ran away.

And she hardly retained at all how much her back had hurt from planting and harvesting beans. She'd worked in the fields throughout childhood and adolescence, even during her first pregnancy and for a few years after, until her mother threw her out of the house, insisting she go to the capital and get a job so the rest of the family could be fed. Her mother had always blamed her for what had happened between María Concepción and her uncle.

"*Ay,*" she moaned. It was monstrous, as if all the skin, from the top of her belly down to her anus, had been torn off and then in the same instant stretched back on. She tried to move her legs, but they were in stirrups. "Push," said the doctor gruffly. "You're not trying, *nena*. Push, or he'll never come out."

"Everything will be all right," the nurse whispered in her ear, "if God wants."

Although he was rough rather than gentle, the doctor had blue eyes like Señor Parra, a friend of the Zorrillas and her cousin's employer. He had been so soothing to her when he made her sign all those papers four months ago. Thinking of him made her feel better, until the pain returned. She winced in agony.

"Try to open up," said the nurse.

But María Concepción couldn't; it hurt so much that, when the baby tried to push his head out of her, she found herself tightening, closing. The baby's will was stronger than hers, however, and she cried out in agony.

The nurse began to massage María Concepción's vagina, to try to soften the muscles and guide the passage of the baby's head. Gripping the sides of the mattress, concentrating with her entire will, María Concepción pushed.

Señor Parra had explained to her that a couple who couldn't have children of their own were not only willing to take care of her baby, but to pay all her hospital expenses, plus 4,000 pesos she could keep for herself. That amount was more than María Concepción earned in three months, more money than she'd ever seen at once. However, as a consequence, she would only be able to see the baby on infrequent occasions.

The arrangement disturbed her. It was a trade-off: once again, her own child would be a distant relative, but at least she'd be sure it was fed. María Concepción only saw her daughter once a year. Angélica, who was now ten, was affectionate during the brief visits, but they hardly knew each other. In any case, it was in God's control, not hers. God had always wanted her to be responsible for her family. Her father had never been much of a provider, and with her uncle gone and her mother so old, with a back too bent to work the fields, someone had to pay the rent for the two-room shack with the dirt floor and corrugated tin roof, for the beans and tortillas.

The doctor looked at his watch and then shook his head. "Give me the scalpel," he told the nurse. "I've got to do an episiotomy." And with a concerted effort, and an overwhelming spasm, María Concepción felt the baby's head finally press out of her, followed by the rest of his body in a liquid charge. Though still in great pain, she felt an intense relief.

It was a boy, with thin black hair matted with blood, round cheeks, pale skin like his father—a *blanquito*. She wanted to take the little thing in her arms. She imagined what an intense joy that would have been, to be able to hold and caress and feed and love her own children.

The *blanquito* began to cry. And as the nurse quickly took him away, María Concepción felt an anguish that was greater not only than the many painful sensations of the past few hours, but of the previous twenty-five years.

★   ★   ★

One Saturday afternoon some nine months earlier, Félix Zorrilla watched television in his bedroom, still wearing the T-shirt and briefs he'd slept in the previous night. He sat up in bed, his legs covered by a blanket. His parents were at their weekend home in Malinalco. "María Concepción!" he cried.

"*Sí, joven,*" called the maid from downstairs.

"Come here!" he shouted.

She had been dusting the glass surfaces of a cabinet in the living room. Sighing, she put down her rag and climbed the stairs. The door to his room was open. "Do you need anything?" she asked. He was watching an episode of her favorite soap opera, about a girl named Cecilia who worked as a clerk in a department store.

His eyes remained glued to the television. "Bring me a Coke," he said.

She walked down the stairs and into the kitchen, filled a tall glass with ice from the automatic machine in the freezer, and then with Coca-Cola from a two-liter plastic bottle. They had ten more such bottles in the closet; the Zorrillas bought them in bulk at Wal-Mart. She ascended the stairs once again, and handed Félix the drink. Eyes on the TV, he accepted the glass wordlessly.

He was watching the lovely Cecilia, in a delicate white night-gown, talking to her elderly father, who worked as the department store's night watchman. They lived in a small but cozy apartment above the premises.

"That's what your mother would have wanted, Cecilia," said the father, smiling kindly under his thick white mustache. "Grand-children."

"*Ay, Papi,*" said Cecilia. "Who would want to marry me?"

"Don't say such things, my beautiful daughter," he said. "Time solves all those questions."

Mesmerized, María Concepción would have loved to stay and

watch the show. But she had to finish the living room, and then clean the bathrooms. She went downstairs.

A few minutes later, as she was polishing the mahogany dining table, she heard Félix's voice again. "María Concepción!"

"Coming," she shouted, and walked up the stairs again. She walked into Félix's room. On television, Ricardo, the dashing son of the owner of the department store, was behind a counter with Cecilia. Ricardo's father was grooming him to take over the business, but was having him learn it from the bottom up, with no special privileges. In fact, Ricardo didn't even use his own name, so the other employees wouldn't know his identity and give him special treatment.

"What a long day," he said to Cecilia with a cap-toothed smile.

"Oh, no," she said, also exposing straight gleaming teeth. María Concepción thought that one of these days she'd like to get her front tooth fixed. "When it's busy the days go by like that," said Cecilia, snapping her fingers.

"What do you need, *joven*?" María Concepción asked.

Eyes on the TV, he handed her the remote control. "Change the channel," he said.

She didn't understand why Félix couldn't change the channel by himself, since all he had to do was press a button. But watching TV beat scrubbing the bathtubs, at least for a couple of minutes. Besides, she liked to use the remote control. When the Zorrillas went away, María Concepción frequently watched TV in Félix's room, changing channels at leisure with the black rectangle. She did it with her heart in her mouth, though: what if it fell apart in her hands? What if the Zorrillas came back unexpectedly early?

She pressed the button. A fat man in a raspberry sport coat and plaid necktie encouraged a giggling contestant to break two eggs over the head of another, who was wearing an orange plastic jumpsuit. "*Rompe los huevos!*" said the announcer, and then "*Ándale!*" as the yolk streamed down the contestant's face.

"*Guácala!*" said Félix. "Change the channel."

María Concepción only had a tiny black-and-white TV in her room, and it was very old. She had to change channels manually.

"Sit down," said Félix. "If you want." He drank from his glass, which María Concepción noticed was still nearly full.

The invitation was unfathomable. "I can't, *joven,*" she said shyly, repressing a smile. "I have work to do."

"Come on, María," said Félix. "Sit down! For a few minutes."

She couldn't help but smile at his audacity. "I can't. I have to work."

"Yes, you can," he said, also smiling. And then, smoothly: "Why don't we make this your work for the moment? You can be my personal channel changer."

She had never spoken much with Félix, but she sort of liked him. He was handsome, more or less, kind of delicate, in a sullen, moody way. She'd never met anyone like him. He was usually quiet, and now suddenly so persuasive. She decided that indulging him for a few minutes wouldn't hurt.

Sitting primly at the edge of the bed, she stared at the television. A thin hawk-faced man in a green double-breasted suit, with lop-sided steel wool hair, placed a microphone in front of the heavily made-up mouth of a young woman with long, dyed auburn tresses. In her mid-twenties, she wore a low-cut black evening dress. María Concepción recognized her; she had played a *muchacha* from the provinces, not unlike herself, in a soap opera a few years back.

"Tell us, Gloria," said the hawk-faced man. "All Mexico wants to know. Are discotheques in Acapulco as much fun as they used to be?"

Gloria screwed up her face in deep reflection. After a long pause, she said, "I don't know. I think they were better before. When I was young. What do you think, Tino?"

"*Qué idiotas,*" said Félix. "Change the channel."

María Concepción obeyed. On the screen, an extremely long and shapely pair of woman's legs, the feet shod in black spike-heeled shoes, emerged from the open door of a shiny blue car. "*Órale!*" said Félix. The camera followed the woman as she stepped from the auto. A statuesque brunette wearing a scoop-necked minidress, she leaned over its hood while the voice of an announcer, trying to sell the vehicle, inventoried its various virtues—its recent vintage, its low mileage, its radio and air-conditioning.

"You want some Coke?" asked Félix.

"No, thank you," said María Concepción.

"*Ándale, nena,*" said Félix. "Enjoy yourself, for once in your life! Don't worry! Go ahead, drink it."

She knew she shouldn't. But he was being so insistent, she wondered if it would be bad manners to refuse. Well, one little sip. She turned and reached for the glass. "Thanks," she said and then tasted the refreshment. She scowled. "It tastes funny."

"What do you mean, funny? There's nothing wrong with it." She stretched her arm to hand it back to him. "Drink some more," he said. "Drink all you like."

She swallowed deeply. It tasted bitter, like the Diet Coke that Señora Zorrilla drank. "Did you put something in this?" she asked.

Félix smiled. "Just a little rum."

María Concepción had never tried rum before. She only drank beer, in small quantities on special occasions with her cousin Eugenia. "I shouldn't drink any more," she said.

"Come on," said Félix. "It's not going to hurt you. I drink it all the time. Have some more."

María Concepción giggled, and took another sip. It wasn't that bad, once you got used to it. She'd have to keep her head. If she drank only a little, scrubbing the bathtubs would pass by quickly, but if she drank a little too much, she wouldn't be able to do them at all. On TV, a smiling woman with dyed blond hair and silicone breasts surfaced from the entrails of a red sports car and stretched her long bare arms to point at its interior. Her dress was so short, María Concepción noticed, that you could almost see her panties. *Qué gata.* The announcer enthusiastically detailed the vehicle's selling points. "The Parras have a car like that," she said. "Where my cousin works."

"Do you like cars?" asked Félix.

She had never been in any except the *señora*'s, when she dropped her off at the market. "Yes," she said.

"Later, we can go for a ride in mine."

"Sure," she said, laughing.

Félix laughed, too. "You know why cars are like women?"

María Concepción drank a little more. She looked at the TV, not at him. "Why?"

"They run smooth after you fill them up."

"That's stupid," she said. But she laughed anyway, at the joke's very witlessness.

"Drink the Coke," said Félix. "Finish it if you want."

"I don't think I better," she said. She realized with alarm that she'd drunk more than half. Well, one more sip wouldn't make a difference.

"Enough with this," he said. "Change the channel again." María Concepción held up the remote control. "No, not with that. I have another *aparato* here."

When she first came to Mexico City to work at the Zorrilla house, María Concepción had been astounded by all the family's possessions. They had soft furniture, scads of clothes they never wore hanging in the closets, electrical appliances the functions of which mystified her, and decorative but completely useless knick-knacks on the shelves and mantels. But in six years, she'd become accustomed to all of that, and didn't think twice when Félix told her he had a second remote control stashed somewhere. She stretched her arm toward him.

"It's here," he said. She leaned farther to reach it, her eyes remaining on the TV. He grabbed her arm and pulled her to him roughly, placing her hand on his penis, which he'd rubbed until it had become erect. "This is my *aparato*."

"Hey!" she said, withdrawing her hand violently. "What are you doing?"

Her sudden vigor aroused him more. "Oh, come on, baby," he said, putting his arms around her. "It's your fault. You did that to me."

"No, Félix," she said, pushing him away. "You're crazy!"

In an instant, he shoved her down and straddled her waist, pinioning her wrists with his hands. The remaining rum-and-Coke spilled; María Concepción felt the cold wetness spread across her lower back. She wondered if it would stain the beige bedspread, and if Señora Zorrilla would blame her. It *was* her fault, for staying and watching TV instead of getting on with her cleaning. "You made me hard because I love you, my darling creature," said Félix, kissing her sloppily on the face and neck.

"Félix, get off of me!" she said, her voice rising in a shriek. She tried to pull out from under him, but he held her down harder. "You're hurting me!"

"I can't help it," he said. "You drive me crazy . . . you know you've tempted me for years, bending over the furniture with your little rag . . . I've loved you for years." He opened his mouth wide and began to suck her throat.

Félix had hardly ever spoken to her beyond a grunt, let alone shown signs that he loved her. Could it be true? María Concepción knew nothing about men, except that you couldn't trust them. Not the ones in her family, anyway, not her sullen father, who drank *mezcal* and refused to plant beans because he said it was women's work, or her uncle who'd raped her. "Stop, Félix," she whimpered, pushing against him, and then submitting as he fumbled with the buttons on her shirt.

She was confused. Filled with a sense that all her days passed uneventfully, this felt like the first time anything had happened to her since she came to Mexico City. She wasn't sure whether it was a good thing, but at least it was *something*. She was also motivated by fear: if she successfully eluded his grasp, she worried Félix would say something bad about her to his mother and that she'd get fired.

As Félix yanked at her bra, María Concepción considered Gloria, who only a couple of years ago had been a maid, but ended up marrying the master of the house—she'd seen it herself on TV. And now she was in a fancy dress, with a new hair color, being interviewed by Tino Mamún. Rich men were different, at least some of them. If Félix wasn't as handsome as Ricardo, the department store heir on the show she liked, he was at least cute. He squeezed her breasts roughly. And sometimes, good things happened to people like María Concepción, who worked hard and stayed out of trouble. She couldn't predict the future, but if she had any money, she'd bet that Ricardo would end up choosing Cecilia, who was poor but good, over his girlfriend, who was wealthy but evil. If he had any sense. She gasped with pain as Félix crudely sucked her nipple. Because it stiffened, he thought he was pleasing her.

Behind the wheel of his Lincoln Town Car, edging out of his driveway, Rogelio Parra looked to the right in preparation for making a left turn. He was abruptly startled by a tapping noise at his window, and his heart began to race. There had been many kidnappings in Las Lomas in the past few years since the peso fell.

But it was only María Concepción, the Zorrillas' *muchacha,* lightly knocking. She must have been stealthily waiting for him; he hadn't seen her at all. He tasted bile that had erupted from his stomach. It was the flavor of fear, an emotion of which he didn't like to be reminded.

He briefly considered ignoring her and driving off. If he did, however, she'd simply return another day. Eugenia, his *muchacha,* had already mentioned two or three times that María Concepción wanted to speak to him. They could be mulish, these *indias.* He pushed a button that opened the passenger-side window.

"Good morning," he said brusquely.

"Good morning, Señor Parra," said María Concepción, looking at the gray-blue carpeting on the floor of the car.

"Can I be of service?" he asked.

She looked up at him with a piteous expression. "Señor Parra, when can I see my baby?" she asked.

Parra sighed. "I can't do anything about that, María Concepción," he said. "I'm sorry. You know those people went back to San Diego. That's where they live. There's nothing I can do. I would help you if I could."

"You said I could see him once in a while."

"Yes. I said you could see him *if possible,*" he said. "But they live in another country. What do you want me to do?"

"Will they ever come back here?" she asked, her voice trembling.

"Well, they might. They probably will. But not in the near future."

Parra felt for the woman. He knew how hard it was for her to relinquish her baby. But he also knew she had no way to care for him properly. And he knew with even deeper conviction that all the babies he arranged to sell to the gringos were better off. They wouldn't suffer the misfortune of growing up in the Mexico of shantytown shacks—victims of poverty, violence, and hunger, and the complete lack of opportunity to better themselves through education, tenacity, or hard work. He earned good money as an adoption lawyer, but he didn't do it for enrichment. He did it for the good of the babies. He was doing them all a favor. He told this to himself every day, and to anyone else who would listen.

"And if I go to San Diego?" asked María Concepción, searching Parra's blue eyes for a sign of hope. "Can I see him then?"

Parra thought she was as likely to get to San Diego as he was to Mars. "Yes, of course," he said. "Anytime you go to San Diego, let me know, and I'll gladly arrange for you to see him." Parra smiled. "Now, if you'll permit me, I have to get to work." He moved his foot off the brake.

"Wait, wait, please, Señor Parra," said María Concepción.

"Yes," he said with impatience.

She was looking at the ground again; merely bringing up the topic filled her with shame. "You said they were going to give me some money."

"Oh, yes," said Parra. "Of course. I'm sure it will arrive any day. I'll make sure you get it at the Zorrillas'. Now, allow me, please—" He left her behind in the Lincoln's exhaust.

"Carolina!" called Carmela Zorrilla.

New *muchachas* were always trouble. The *señora* resigned herself to a long period of struggle after hiring the seventeen-year-old *morenita,* just arrived in Mexico City from some godforsaken settlement in Guerrero. For instance, a friend called a few days earlier to let Carmela know that when Carolina answered the phone, not only did she refuse to take messages, she hung up unceremoniously. This unnerved Carmela to no end, but she realized she must have patience: it was simply a matter of teaching telephone etiquette to an ignorant peasant who'd never lived with a phone before. That was easier, however, than teaching her how to write down the names of the people who called—Carolina barely knew the alphabet.

Her husband ate lunch in restaurants more often, because he claimed he didn't like Carolina's food. Again, this was a matter of enlightening someone who had subsisted all her life on a diet of beans, tortillas, and on special occasions, potato chips. She would learn how to cook real food, but not overnight.

At least someone was satisfied. "This soup is delicious," said Félix.

"Don't slurp, my son," she said.

"Sorry, *mamá*," he said.

A fount of affection for her darling *niño* welled up in Carmela. He was a dutiful son to her, even if he sometimes disobeyed his father. She rued the day he would marry and leave home; it would be so dreadfully quiet without him.

Carmela wondered what had gone wrong with María Concepción. It simply wouldn't have done to have a *muchacha* with a baby—she couldn't care for an infant and work at the same time. Abortions were of course prohibited by the church, not to mention against the law of the land. Yet she didn't want to be so crude as to fire the girl.

She thought she'd done María Concepción an important favor by connecting her with Señor Parra, but after the baby was born, the girl had strangely drifted off into space. When Carmela had finally commented that something seemed to be the matter, María Concepción had given her a blank look and then disappeared the day after payday, never to be heard from again. It was a shame. But that seemed to be the disease of the *muchachas:* they functioned for a few years, and then one disaster or another befell them, like becoming impregnated by some *burro,* some spineless cowardly *naco.* Then they vanished, and you had to start all over again.

Carmela noticed that the salsa was not on the table. "Carolina!" she cried.

"*Sí, señora?*" Short, perpetually smiling, with apple cheeks, her black hair tied back, Carolina entered the room, drying her hands on a towel tucked into her skirt. She stopped after two steps, and swallowed something she had been chewing. Like her cheeks, her breasts and behind were round, but they were obscured to Carmela's satisfaction by loose clothing.

"The green sauce, Carolina," said Carmela. "We serve it with every meal. Breakfast, lunch, and dinner."

"*Ay, perdón,*" said Carolina, smacking her forehead with the flat of her hand and giggling. She was sweet, thought Carmela, but her honeyed charm wouldn't go all that far if she kept forgetting things.

Carmela looked from the maid to her discreetly leering son, and back again, and gasped. Suddenly her heart began to pound. By then Carolina was already back to the kitchen getting the sauce.

The second-class bus was ancient, suffocating, and reeked of sweat and diesel. Every seat was occupied and the aisle was crammed with standees, many of whom carried bulging cardboard boxes tied with twine. A couple of passengers bore livestock.

The ride had been jolting, but without incident, until the vehicle broke down an hour north of Guadalajara. It was a cool, crisp December afternoon, and the surrounding mountain range was majestic in the spectacularly unclouded sunlight.

The passengers who had seats stayed in them, while most of the standees, along with the driver and the ticket taker, stepped outside and stood on the edge of the road. In the brisk air, the majority of the people idled, their hands behind their backs, shifting their weight from one foot to another. A few of the more enterprising squatted beside the vehicle and quizzically stared at the entrails underneath.

The lean, stone-faced driver, with sunglasses and a mustache, simply stood there, his arms folded, a lit cigarette in his mouth. They could gawk all they wanted; neither God nor the devil would get the bus moving. He had no radio to communicate with the dispatcher. It made no difference to him; he'd climb on the next bus, scheduled to pass by in two hours. It would be crowded, too; unfortunately, the poor bastards who had been his passengers wouldn't get where they'd been going until who knew when. They got what they deserved for trying to save a few pennies by going second class, or simply for being poor bastards.

María Concepción waited with the other standees alongside the bus for half an hour, but soon became spooked with the notion that she'd never get anywhere this way, envisioning herself still waiting there in a week's time, on Christmas Day. Idly, she began to walk north along the highway. Soon, after a bend in the road, she lost sight of the bus and its passengers. No cars came in either direction; it was truly the middle of nowhere. She patted the secret pocket in her skirt, where she had deposited eleven hundred tightly folded pesos, almost all of her last month's salary. She never did get the money from Señor Parra, and gave up asking for it after a few months.

It was a little scary, but also exhilarating to be alone surrounded by the mountains, away from everyone. It was cold, though, and soon would be dark. After a while, a northbound pickup truck screeched to a stop at her side. "Where you going?" asked a smiling young man in the passenger seat. He wore a clean shirt and a cap with the Dallas Cowboys logo on its forehead.

"San Diego," she said.

"*Híjole,*" said the young man, his fingers drumming on the door. "We're only going as far as Santiago Ixcuintla, but climb in the back if you want."

She looked at the cab of the truck. Atop a pile of wood chips sat an elderly toothless man, with a wrinkled leathery face, who carried two strings, attached to the necks of two gobbling turkeys, fattened for Christmas. There was also a man in his thirties, unshaven, run to fat, wearing a straw hat and a fake leather jacket. She clambered in cautiously, making sure that her skirt didn't hike much above her knobby knees as she ascended.

The landscape, with the sun just beginning to set over the mountains, was stunning, but as soon as the truck found its pace, a frigid wind chilled María Concepción. She lifted the collar of her denim jacket and hugged herself, but it didn't make much of a difference in temperature.

The unshaven man scrutinized her: pretty, but a bit hard. "Going to San Diego?" he asked. María Concepción nodded. "It's far away," he said.

"Just so long as I get there by Christmas," she said.

She'll get there when pigs fly, thought the man. He smiled. "It's cold, no?" he said. María Concepción didn't respond. She looked toward the elderly man. His eyes were open, but he seemed to be asleep, or dead.

"*Nena,*" said the unshaven man. "Why don't I come over there? I'll sit next to you. With the two of us together, we can warm things up a little, no?"

"*Chinga tu madre,*" said María Concepción viciously. "If you touch me, I swear I'll kill you.'' The man looked at her as if she had escaped from an insane asylum. Good, she thought. She'd have to be tough if she was ever going to make it to the United States, because the road was going to be full of *cabrones* like him. Men are shit, she thought. The two turkeys made gobbling noises, and stumbled atop the wood chips. She looked at them, and felt a familiar sensation: hunger.

TAXI

*i*n the backseat of the Volkswagen Beetle, the woman, her baggy eyes shut, chants the Lord's Prayer over and over. She's sitting in between The Monkey, who has a simian arm casually draped over her shoulder, as if he were her boyfriend, and Handsome, who is rifling through the contents of her purse. I can see through the rearview mirror that he's found her wallet.

"Your name's Lourdes," he says, reading from her driver's license. "Lourdes Santos de Díaz. What do you know, you live in Las Lomas! At 2721 Sierra Gorda."

The recitation of her name and address doesn't break her concentration, not even for a second. She continues to drone the Lord's Prayer. It's starting to get on my nerves. I bet she hasn't been in a church in years, except for weddings and communions. But once in my taxi, most of the "passengers" put on a big show of piety.

I look at her in the rearview mirror. Her face, slack with middle age, is grimly set. I return my gaze to the road. "Lourdes?" I ask. "Are you a religious woman?"

"Yes," she says. She smoothes down her beige skirt, as if any of us were interested in her legs. "Yes, I am."

"Good," I counter. "Then not only will God protect you, he will pay you back threefold anything we take from you."

Handsome goes through her husband's wallet. "And your name is Adolfo," he says. Adolfo is lying in a fetal position on the floor of the cab, where the passenger seat has been removed so people can get in and out more easily. He chokes, gasping, yet again. The Monkey stretches his leg and places his big foot in the crack of Adolfo's ass, just to make sure he doesn't get carried away. "Please," says Adolfo in a strained voice. "Please, let us go, for the love of God." I can't stand it when they beg. I am by no means a violent person, but the whining makes me want to move my foot from the accelerator and stomp their faces.

"You've got everything we have," says Lourdes, finally taking a break from praying. "Our money, his wallet, my purse. The amethyst chain that my mother gave me. You even have our wedding rings! There's nothing else you can take from us. When will you let us go?"

"In a little while we're going to pick up our colleague," I say. "If you give us the correct PIN numbers to your credit cards we'll release you as soon as we get some cash." I pause for dramatic effect. "If you don't, we'll kill you."

This last bit is pure bluff. My associates and I have been working the same routine for a year and we haven't killed anyone yet. It's true we've had to rough up some particularly stubborn customers, but only to get them to cooperate. We're not out for blood; we need money. And there aren't many ways to get it these days.

"My husband has a heart condition," Lourdes whines. "He left his medicine at home."

"I know, I know," I say. "Don't worry, Lourdes. If you obey, you'll be going home very soon."

By my estimation, Adolfo's heart condition, like Lourdes's religious devotion, is a fairy tale. If my "passengers" are to be believed, every man in Mexico City is sick. If he doesn't have a bad
heart, he's got asthma, cancer, AIDS, or some new disease I've
never even heard of that's highly contagious. And wouldn't you
know it, they've always left their medicine at home. Some of them,
like Adolfo here, gasp subtly, while others do such an exaggerated
coughing-wheezing-and-moaning act that you want to drop them
off at Televisa so they can audition for a soap opera.

"Please," repeats Adolfo. "Please let us go."

"Shut your mouth already!" says The Monkey intensely, pressing down the foot that's up Adolfo's ass.

"Don't hurt us!" whimpers Lourdes, her face turning red. Her
white-knuckled fists are just above her knees, at the hem of her
skirt. "Whatever you do, please don't hurt us! My husband is a
sick man!"

"We won't hurt you, Lourdes," I say. "We won't even touch
you. As long as you do what we say." Quiet finally settles in the
taxi.

I want to make sure they stay hushed for a while, so I go into
a speech that usually has a tranquilizing effect. "There's one thing
I want to make clear," I say. "We are not to blame for what's
happening to you. It's the government's fault. Mexico has turned
its back on the Mexicans, and forced us to steal to live." I can feel
their disgust. This polemic will buy us about five minutes of silence.

I didn't always do this. I used to be a working stiff. I spent nearly
ten years at the Central de Abastos, managing two stands, selling
fruits and vegetables. Every day the guy who owned them would
drop in once or twice—to check up on me—but I did all the
work for him.

I was a trustworthy employee. I got paid a hundred pesos a day and only skimmed an extra hundred or so off the top. I'm sure the boss knew about it. It was enough for some extras for my kids, but not so much that he would raise a stink. Some people who work in the market rob the owners blind. Not me.

Then they devalued the peso. From one day to the next, the value of my hundred pesos was cut in half. The boss refused to give me a raise, so I quit. Actually, it was a little more complicated: after he turned down my request for an increase, I started to help myself to more of his profits, and he got wise pretty fast. When he accused me of stealing, I was forced to leave. It was a question of honor.

So I started to drive a taxi. A beautiful job! I walk in the garage in the afternoon, hand over a hundred pesos to the fleet manager, and then go out in the world, competing with thousands of other cabs for five- and ten-peso fares. It takes a good five hours to earn back the hundred. Then I have to pay for gas and lunch. If I work all night, I might come home at dawn with a hundred, a hundred and twenty-five pesos. If I'm lucky. I've got three kids to feed.

I was talking about how rough things are to Handsome, who's my wife's brother. He used to be with the *judiciales,* the plain-clothes police—the kings of thieves, the criminal elite. He also got fired a short while ago, during a corruption sweep. So he proposed we go into business together. The whole robbery scenario was his idea.

I picked up Lourdes and Adolfo about fifteen minutes earlier, fol-lowing the usual routine. I cruise the big streets in the nice neigh-borhoods while a five-year-old gray Shadow, bearing my three accomplices—The Monkey, Handsome, and Manuel—follows at a respectful distance.

I only pick up well-dressed, prosperous-looking people: couples or men alone. Usually they're *güeros:* in this country, the whiter you are, the richer you are.

A couple of minutes later, when I stop at a red light, The Monkey and Handsome jump out of the Shadow and barrel into the taxi. They both squeeze into the backseat—it's so tight that Handsome is practically in Lourdes's lap. They announce that they're federal judicial police looking for drugs, and order me to keep driving. Manuel, still in the Shadow, stays on their tail.

The couple normally knows from the jump that The Monkey and Handsome are no more policemen than they are mariachis. But by the time the door is shut, it's too late: they're our prisoners, cozily crammed in the backseat.

The Monkey of course gets his nickname because he looks like a gorilla. An enormous, ominous goon, he dresses in a track suit and sneakers. On top of this, he brandishes a knife. As he threatens our "passengers," Handsome divests them of their jewelry, purses, watches, and wallets. (Despite his nickname, Handsome is in fact quite ugly, but wears a dark suit and tie, gets his shoes shined regularly, and keeps his hair cut short, giving him the look of a proper little bank clerk.)

Usually the male of the couple makes at least a show of being a *machito* by raising his voice or pushing around in his seat. Old Adolfo claimed a relationship with a high functionary in the Secretariat of the Interior, and threatened severe repercussions if we didn't let them go immediately.

In response, The Monkey will stick his knife toward a throat or slap a face. In this case, he twisted Adolfo's arm as if he had been wringing out a wet dishrag, until his nice sport jacket began to tear at the seam of the sleeve. That was enough to put Adolfo in his place, but just in case, we made him lie down on the floor of the cab, where he could get a good view of our shoes and smell the metal and gasoline.

Handsome goes through the couples' wallets. This is where we all start to call them by their first names, and comment on what a nice neighborhood they live in. Which tends to spook them sufficiently to give up the PIN numbers to their credit cards.

Handsome is playing with three or four cards in his hand. "Adolfo," he says. "What's the PIN number to your Banamex Visa here?"

With another little gasp, Adolfo says, "forty-eight-zero-four." You can usually tell when someone comes clean with a number: they say it immediately, right off the bat.

"And Lourdes," he says, practically whispering in her ear. "This one from Bancomer?"

She whimpers. "I can't think of it," she says in a high-pitched whine.

If they take a long time trying to come up with it, or say they forgot, they're usually lying. The Monkey knows his cue. "Give me the fucking number, *cabrona*! Or I'll kill your husband!" He leans over, placing his knife against Adolfo's ear.

"Tell him, *gorda,*" says Adolfo.

Continuing to snivel, Lourdes ekes out, "ninety-five seventy-three."

"Don't lie!" says Handsome. "We want the real number!" To a certain extent, he can be persuasive as well—he's got a gruff voice. The problem is stature. Handsome is so tiny that his effect is rather like a barking poodle's. The Monkey really carries the weight here.

"I swear, that's it," moans Lourdes. "Ninety-five seventy-three."

"And what about this one from Banca Confía?"

Getting PIN numbers is tricky. Sometimes people truly forget them—because they just use the cards to buy things, and not to withdraw cash. We had a lot to learn in the beginning. The Monkey kicked several asses to no avail, for instance, before we found out that you can't even get cash from an ATM with an American Express card. We don't bother to take those anymore.

After we get the cards, we stop at a quiet side street in Xochimanca. Handsome, in his neat little bank teller's suit and tie, leaves us, takes over the Shadow, and drives around trying to take out cash from the ATMs. Manuel—The Monkey's tall and skinny cousin, who never cracks a smile—comes into our car to add his threatening presence.

I cruise along the expressways, either the Periférico or the Circuito Interior—no stop lights, no cops, and at this hour, no traffic either. If everything goes according to plan, we're all back in Xochimanca a few thousand pesos richer in half an hour, and the couple gets dumped safe and sound on the sidewalk.

But our routine is just as likely to work out badly as well. For instance, sometimes the ATM computers are down and you have to wait a long time before they give up any money. This can go on for an hour or more. An ambiguous message will keep popping up on the screen: "Unable to provide service at this time." Sometimes it's true, sometimes it's the wrong PIN number. This is when The Monkey has to kick a little ass to persuade them to give us the right numbers.

Some people who work this routine go to the houses of the "passengers" and rob them. But that's a risky ploy. Rich people's neighborhoods are crawling with silent burglar alarms and gunslinging security guards. With the alarms, you typically end up in jail; if you're caught by a guard, either he turns you in, shoots you in the balls, or makes you split the booty with him. And you never know who's going to be at home, or whether they have a weapon around. If by some miracle you go through all this effort unharmed, you can still find there isn't very much cash in the house.

And if you don't get cash, you're fucked. It gets tougher every day to fence anything profitably. We know a few hardnoses in Tepito who'll give us a half-decent price for jewelry. But just try passing off a set of silver or a VCR! Everyone knows where you got it and how desperate you are. It's criminal. You assume all the risk and get pennies for your trouble. The fences are ruthless, but it's not their fault—nobody's buying anything from them, either. Everyone's broke these days.

Sometimes we end up with nothing at all from the credit cards, having wasted an hour and a half of everyone's time and a few liters of gas. Nevertheless, the cards are still your best possibility of maximizing your profit. Occasionally, when we score with the ATMs, we score big. Once, we got two thousand pesos apiece from five different cards. That was a good night. It felt like winning the lottery.

And for all anyone cares, we could be driving around with these stiffs in the cab all night or even all week. It's not as if there are any police around looking to stop us. They're far too busy working their own shakedowns: the suckers they catch for traffic violations, or the kids necking in parked cars, or the fags coming out of the bars in the Zona Rosa.

This is the way it works. You go for the biggest score as fast as possible, no matter the risks. Just a few months ago, they caught our previous president's sister-in-law trying to withdraw $84 million from a Swiss bank account. Her husband stole all that working for CONASUPO, a government program that's supposed to help the poor. If he got $84 million, how much do you think his brother got in the six years he was president?

Almost an hour later, and no sign of Handsome in our assigned corner in Xochimanca. He must be having trouble getting money from the cash machines. Lourdes has been buzzing out the Lord's Prayer again for the last fifteen minutes. Adolfo suddenly lets out a big wheeze and a smothered cough.

"Please," whines Lourdes, "my husband has a heart condition." She has sung that tune maybe six times in the last hour; "My Husband's Heart," along with the Lord's Prayer and "When Will You Let Us Go," will one day be compiled in a CD of her greatest hits.

"Don't worry," I say. "You'll be going home very soon."

"Listen," says Adolfo. He continues in a slow, strangled voice: "You said that what's happening to us isn't your fault, that it's because of the government. Okay. But *we're* not the government. See what I'm saying?" He coughs. "My wife and I are ordinary citizens. We never did anything to you, we never took anything from you."

I look at the man on the floor: his gray mustache, his moist, imploring brown eyes, his torn sport coat. He has a point; he's hardly the first "passenger" to make it. But let's face it: even if he isn't in the government, it's hard to feel sorry for him. He lives in Las Lomas. You don't make it to that neighborhood with clean hands. There are probably more servants living in his house than members of his own family.

Meanwhile, I live in Meyehualco in a square concrete box under a tin roof. I've got one of the only houses on the street that has a real floor; most of my neighbors walk on dirt.

"Well, my friend," I tell him, "it's your turn. Your number

came up." But my curiosity is piqued. "So if you're not with the government, Adolfo, what about your buddy in the Secretariat of the Interior?"

"He's a nobody," says Adolfo grimly. "Just a hack with the PRI. I mentioned him because I thought you'd let us go."

Lourdes starts to whimper, saying, "Please. We've got two daughters and three grandchildren."

"Since my father died," gasps Adolfo, "my mother depends on me. I'm all she's got."

"We've all got mothers, we've all got children," I say. "I've got three little girls."

"*Viejo,*" says The Monkey, tapping Adolfo's ass with his foot. "If you don't work for the PRI, what do you do?"

"Me?" asks Adolfo. "I'm with the phone company."

Manuel and the Monkey start to laugh. "*Hijo de su puta madre!* You're the biggest thieves of all!" says Manuel. "My mother applied for a phone a year ago and she still hasn't got a line!"

"Nonsense," says Adolfo. "There are over ninety thousand new lines available in the city!"

"Sure, we've all seen the ads," I say. "Somehow you seem to get them a lot faster if you pay a fat bribe under the table. My phone's been out of order for three months and they keep promising me they'll fix it *mañana.*"

"That's very perplexing," says Adolfo, suddenly excited. "Those days are supposed to be over, but I suppose there are still a few bad apples in *Teléfonos de México.* You know, I've been working there many years, and have a certain amount of influence. I could get your mother a line, and fix your phone, too."

"Sure, *viejo,*" says The Monkey, laughing. "We'll give you our names and addresses and you can come over with your tool box."

Where the hell is Handsome? I've passed by our corner five times in the last hour and he's nowhere in sight. Probably, he's just having trouble getting cash from the machines, but it's getting a little too snug for me in this cab.

Manuel appears to have read my mind. No sooner are we back on the Periférico than he asks, "What happened to your little *compadre?*"

I ignore the remark. "He should have been there by now," says The Monkey.

"He'll be there, *okay?*" I say as sharply as I can. It doesn't help anyone to get rattled and argue in the car.

"You don't think he's getting any ideas, do you?" asks Manuel. I always thought he could be counted on at least to keep his mouth shut.

"What do you mean?" I ask.

"I mean to keep the money for himself!"

"Are you crazy?" I snarl.

"Don't call me crazy, get it?" he asks. "I'm just wondering if he's charging us a commission is all."

"Would you tell your cousin to shut up?" I ask The Monkey.

"If you want me to shut up, tell me yourself," says Manuel.

"Maybe you're working together with him," says The Monkey. "He's your brother-in-law, after all."

"Enough!" I shout. "We'll talk about it later!"

Adolfo inhales sharply. "Could you let us go while you discuss these matters?" Lourdes cries. "Please, I swear, we gave you our real numbers."

"We'll let you go soon," I say.

"You're damn right we'll talk," says Manuel.

I'm so rattled that I don't even notice the speed bump in my path and bang right over it, rocking the taxi as if a bomb had exploded inside. Adolfo bounces like a rubber ball, Lourdes screams, and The Monkey slaps her across the face, which just makes her scream louder. Manuel practically falls off the seat.

"Everyone shut up!" I shout, and to my surprise they follow my directions.

Suddenly, Adolfo begins to jerk around on the floor. "He needs his medicine," Lourdes says breathlessly. "Please take us home so he can have his medicine. We have money in the house! I have jewelry. I have clothes. You can have my car! You can have it all! He needs his medicine now!"

This sounds like a pretty good offer. But Las Lomas is full of those stinking guards and burglar alarms. It could be a trap; just thinking about it gives me the shivers.

"*Órale,*" says The Monkey finally. "Let's go."

"Wait a minute," I say. "You're crazy."

"Let's go!" says The Monkey. "To Las Lomas, *cabrón.* Where do you live, Sierra Gorda?"

"You're out of line!" I shout.

"Shut up and drive!" shouts Manuel, louder than me. "We're going to Lomas!" I guess I'm outvoted.

As it happens, we're not very far. "What's the exit?" I sigh. "Alencastre or Reforma?"

"Palmas," says Lourdes. Even closer.

The Monkey is talking to Adolfo in a low menacing voice. "And you better not try anything stupid, my friend. Your wife made us a nice, hospitable offer. We're going to take her up on it. This is between her and us, you get it?" Lourdes is sobbing quietly. "You get it? Because if you don't, you're dead." He gives Adolfo a quick little kick in the ass. The man just jerks limply.

"Look, he's asleep," says The Monkey, laughing. He bends over and starts to shake Adolfo. "Wake up, *cabrón,*" he says. The man lies there inert. His eyes have rolled back; his trap is open with what looks like a shocked expression. Lourdes has her hand over her mouth. "*Híjole,*" says The Monkey.

I'm already cruising down Palmas. "What number Sierra Gorda is your house?" I ask. Lourdes just sits there looking at her husband, or what's left of him, her hand over her mouth.

"Answer him," says Manuel.

With great effort, she says, "Twenty-seven twenty-one."

My heart is pounding. Driving along looking for their house, the next couple of minutes pass by like an hour. Luckily they live on a dark section of the street.

I stop the car, and The Monkey gets out. He pulls Adolfo by the legs until the body is halfway on the sidewalk, then reaches inside and grabs him by the collar and arm. There's a tearing sound as the sleeve of his sport jacket separates from the body.

Clumsily, The Monkey drags Adolfo's corpse along the sidewalk and drops it in front of the gate, like one of those ten-peso sacks of oranges they sell from the back of a truck. You can see the whites of his eyes and his tongue is hanging out.

"Don't make a sound," Manuel tells Lourdes, who is whimpering quietly, the back of her hand against the cheek where The Monkey smacked her.

I turn and look at her. "Take off your shoes," I said.

"No," she says in a hysterical whisper.

"Come on, Lourdes. Take them off."

"You're going to rape me!" she says.

"What?" I ask.

"Please, don't rape me," she cries. I look at Manuel, who covers his smile with his hand.

"Nobody's going to rape anybody, Lourdes," I say. "I just want your shoes so you don't run after us." She looks at me as if I've spoken in a foreign language, but then gets the idea and slips off her pumps. "When you get out of the car," I say, "go straight to your husband. Don't turn back and look at us. If you do, you're dead."

Meanwhile, The Monkey's just standing there like he's waiting for the bus. "Get in," I say.

"What? I'm going inside with her."

"Well, that's great, *pendejo,* because you're going in alone. I'm getting out of here."

"He's right," says Manuel, "get in."

He climbs in the backseat, muttering about our lack of balls. As I pull away, I see Lourdes in the rearview mirror bending over Adolfo's body, stretching the beige fabric of her skirt.

I'm cruising down Palmas. "Let me see the chain," I tell The Monkey.

"What chain?" he says.

"*No mames, cabrón,*" I say. "The one with the purple stones. The one she said was her mother's."

"Oh, that chain. Handsome got the chain."

"Don't lie. I saw you put it in your pocket."

"So what!" he says. "It's my turn. That's my girlfriend's chain, get it?"

I get it, all right. Actually, it's my turn, but I don't feel like arguing right now.

A BEACH DAY

*P*eter hated the May weather, just before the rainy season, a teeming humidity mixed with blast-furnace heat that felt like walking through boiling water. He hated the litter—used diapers and cellophane candy wrappers, papaya peels, and empty plastic Coke bottles—strewn all over the sidewalks. He hated the intoxicating stench of the diesel fuel, and the black smoke gushing from exhaust pipes straight into his face. The rank odor had followed him and Deborah from the enormous and chaotic capital, where they'd started their trip, to the colonial town with the famous cathedral, and finally here to the beach.

He hated the poverty—the workers squatting on their haunches outside the cathedral, signs advertising the availability of their daily labor; the stooped and ancient shoeshine men with their broken-toothed smiles of servility; the Indian women seated on the sidewalk, with extended arms, palms up, always a suckling baby at the brown and wrinkled breast.

Nothing Peter had seen in London, where he grew up; in Europe, where he'd traveled extensively; or in New York, where he

now lived, had prepared him for the persistent sense of loathing
he felt in Mexico. In fact, he hadn't anticipated anything, since all
he knew about the country to which he'd agreed to accompany
Deborah on a ten-day vacation were the predictable clichés of heat,
laziness, and Yankee imperialism.

He hated everything he saw, but if there was anything he hated
most of all, it was the guns, and the blank-eyed, dark-skinned boys
who carried them. There weren't teeming masses of them, but just
enough armed police and soldiers around to make Peter feel uneasy. They were like an overly repetitive motif, the melody of an
obnoxious song played constantly on the radio.

The evening that he and Deborah arrived in the capital, a platoon of rifle-bearing servicemen were on drill in the plaza, marching in formation. Later that night, some of them leaned against the
dense stone walls of the colonial buildings, cigarettes stuck between
their heavy lips. Peter could make out the flatness of their bellies
and the sinewy muscles under the starched polyester khakis, and
the insinuating way their gloomy eyes followed Deborah's round
and swerving bottom.

Two days later, arriving in the cathedral town, he noticed the
pair of cops standing guard outside the bank, bearing junior machine guns that matched their compact stature. One held his
weapon with two hands across his belly, while the other balanced
his against his shoulder. In addition to the guns, they wore bullet-
proof vests. Despite the air-conditioning inside the bank, Peter
sweated heavily as he waited for Deborah to cash a traveler's check.

Even here at Puerto de los Santos, the sleepy beach resort, Peter
spotted a sinister *uniformado,* pistol in a holster at his hip, silently
pop into a boutique, lower his mirrored sunglasses, and survey the
bronzed and oiled flesh of the female tourists, who wore little to
cover their swimsuits as they shopped for towels, jewelry, and sou-

venirs. He'd seen several of the men stiffly wandering along the concrete embankment in their combat boots, the sea breeze spraying their inscrutable faces.

Peter looked at Deborah, lying on her stomach atop an enormous rectangle of amber terry cloth. Covering her ripe mango of a behind was a pink bikini bottom beginning to lose its elasticity. (The same could not be said of Deborah's thirty-two-year-old form, which, although leaning toward plumpness, was conditioned three times a week in a body-building gym in midtown.) Peter followed the slow rise and fall of her torso.

"You might want to put on a bit more suntan lotion," he said. "The sun is quite strong." He had not meant to sound so fussy and felt embarrassed. His own gangly body was mostly covered by a baggy yellow T-shirt and antediluvian jeans cut off at the knees.

"Put it on me," said Deborah. Her voice was deep and throaty, but not sultry; she sounded more like a twelve-year-old with bronchitis than Lauren Bacall. Peter put the sunscreen, gluey, white, and redolent of coconut, on the bony fingers of his left hand and gingerly spread it on his palms. He truly hated the way these gooey unguents invariably mixed with sand; the compound got under your fingernails and couldn't be removed without a vigorous scrubbing in soap and water. Carefully, as if she were made of thin glass, he distributed the salve along her flushed and perspiring back, stopping when he got to the enfeebled band of her bikini, riding atop the crack of her backside. "Mmmm," she said. "Do my legs, too, Peter."

He pretended not to hear this last remark. "There goes another of the banditos," he said, looking at a policeman walking along the *malecón*. This one, he noticed, had a pot belly and a black mustache, and moved with particular slowness.

"Not again, Peter," Deborah said, groaning. "Why are you obsessed with the cops? Most of them are just kids. They're so skinny they swim inside those uniforms."

"Yes, exactly," said Peter. "They're impetuous adolescents. Which makes them all the more dangerous."

"Being a cop or soldier is an ugly job," said Deborah. "Most people who do it don't have a lot of other choices."

Peter countered by opening Deborah's guidebook and reading aloud a brief passage that mentioned the police's legendary reputation for occasionally shaking down a tourist. Common ploys were to invent a traffic violation to exact a bribe from a driver, or to sell marijuana to a mark and then arrest him for its possession. There was even the uncommon episode of exceptionally brutal violence—the book mentioned the rape and robbery of an elderly American couple by patrol cops along the highway a few years back. But that was up north, by the border—drug-trafficking territory. Peter neglected to read the paragraph explaining that these incidents were assured to be few, with most tourists passing through not only unmolested but blissfully happy.

"This is my third time in Mexico," Deborah said. "I've always minded my own business, and somehow, miraculously, nothing bad has ever happened to me."

Naturally not, thought Peter. Deborah seemed to feel that Mexico was a Disney movie in Technicolor unfolding for her alone. In the past days, he'd grown increasingly irritated as she merrily chirped on about the burnt and leathery food accompanied by violently peppery sauces, the gloomy thick-stoned colonial architecture, and especially the decaying pre-Columbian ruins. All Peter saw among those sites were gaggles of sweating and groaning tourists, yet Deborah ranted on about the asinine pictures that entered her mind (slaves carrying boulders across their backs to build pyramids; literally heart-wrenching human sacrifices), and the grave sense of history they inspired in her.

She also tended to natter on about the individuals she referred to as "the people," such as the tiresome youths who'd shared her and Peter's café table in the plaza, eager to practice their fractured English, and the monotonously sycophantic waiters, chambermaids, and desk clerks. If most of "the people" in the country were poor, Deborah opined that they nonetheless seemed reasonably happy, taking joy in small pleasures—like the wretched smudge-faced mother and her infant son on the wheezing second-class bus that had transported them from the town to the beach. The pair had been sitting with expressions of absolute gratification, sharing a lethally yellow drink from a plastic bag tied at the top, with a straw stuck inside.

Peter didn't understand how anyone could take pleasure in Mexico at all. His indignation had begun on the plane, when the airline charged three dollars for the whiskey he drank. The fact that Deborah paid made it no less of an outrage. As soon as they landed in the capital, there was a mix-up with baggage, as eager but useless handlers removed all the suitcases from the conveyor belt and put them in an enormous disorganized pile from which it became agonizing to unearth one's own.

"They're all mad here," Peter decided then and there, and that was how he continued to refer to nearly everyone they encountered—taxi drivers, shopgirls, waiters—if not "mad" they were "nutters," "barking" or in the best of cases "dim." When they visited museums, he found little worth looking at, except for the canvases of two or three artists whose names he recognized. The cathedrals, he griped, paled when contrasted with those in Europe. A harmless walk along the streets would turn him into a stinging architectural critic, and when they escaped the heat inside a cantina, the beer, despite its international fame, was either too cold, too fizzy, or simply insipid.

"Innocent lads, indeed." Peter tittered as he watched the policeman disappear in the distance. "I wouldn't trust that one for a minute. He'd nick your socks without taking your shoes off."

"The people have treated you nicely," said Deborah. "No one's tried to take anything from you."

"Deborah," he groaned, responding like an imperious nanny to the sore-throated child in her voice. "Why do you imagine they carry guns in the first place? Either they're set to rob you or kill you or both. Just looking at them makes me uneasy."

Playa Tranquila, where they lay, had the grayest sand, and was the most littered and least lovely beach in Puerto de los Santos, but it had the virtue of being smack in the middle of downtown, unlike the prettier seascapes, which required a bus or taxi to reach. Indeed, Peter and Deborah were sunning themselves a mere fifty paces from where they were staying, the Hotel Florecita, in an enormous twenty-dollar room with terra-cotta tiles and a broken ceiling fan, that smelled of the sea and resounded with the crash of the waves hitting the shore.

They were alone. Few foreigners came to Puerto de los Santos in the off-season, and the Mexican tourists wouldn't drift in until the weekend. Deborah sat up, pulled her arms out from the straps of her bikini's bra, and pulled it down to the tops of her nipples, to tan as much of her body as possible. She lay down on her back. Peter, beginning to feel restless, marveled at her immobility. He looked at the little arc of her belly, turning redder under the sun's glare, and the V of her pink bikini bottom, from under which, to his disapproval, disorderly blond curls had materialized. He scratched a knobby knee and ran lank fingers through his fine black hair.

"Hello, amigos!" a voice called out behind them.

They turned around. A man of about thirty, in filthy jeans and a gray shirt so rumpled it appeared he'd worn it for several days, staggered over to them and dropped to the sand, exhaling heavily after landing. His jet black hair was lavishly oily and unkempt, and he hadn't shaved since he'd put on the shirt. He smelled not only unwashed, but as if the entire contents of a bottle of rum, locally concocted and retailing for three dollars, had recently been up-turned over his head.

"Hello," said Deborah, putting her arms through her bra straps and attempting to remove the sand that had sprayed her shoulders with the man's jolting arrival. Peter ignored him.

"Welcon' to my country," he said.

"Thank you," said Deborah.

"You like it here?"

"Oh, we love it," she said, deciding to speak for both.

"My names Carlos," he said. "Wha's your names?"

"I'm Deborah and that's Peter," she said. Peter noted that Deborah always spoke with excruciating slowness to "the people," to make sure they understood her.

Carlos's eyes remained fixed on Deborah. "Where you fron, Deborah?" he asked. He suddenly redistributed his body and in the process inadvertently kicked more sand on Peter.

"New York," said Deborah.

"New Yor!" Carlos exclaimed, looked at the sky, and let out a laugh, as if he'd been told a joke. "*Las torres gemelas,*" he said enthusiastically.

"What?" she asked.

"The towers twins," said Carlos, raising his arms.

"Oh, the World Trade Center," she said.

"*Sí,* the Word Tray Center," said Carlos eagerly. "The most tallest buildings in the word. One day I go there."

Peter didn't understand why Deborah had to engage in senti-mental chatter with every chambermaid, juice vendor, urchin, and malingerer who crossed their path. Americans, he thought, are so tiresome in their desire to be liked. He noticed that this particular derelict had a bloody bruise at the corner of his mouth, as if he'd been struck in a barroom melee. He was skeptical about the man's assertion that he'd been to New York. "Did you quite like it?" Peter asked him.

Carlos considered Peter for the first time, and from the expression on his face, didn't think much of what he saw. "*Qué dices?*" he asked.

"Did you quite like it? Did you like New York?" Peter asked impatiently.

"No, Peter," said Deborah. "He'd like to go."

"*Sí,* I like to go," said Carlos, encouraged by Deborah. "I like to go to the most tallest buildings in the word."

"You went to the top, did you?" asked Peter.

"He didn't go, Peter," said Deborah, her voice deepening even further. "He *hopes* to go, some day."

"Yes, I have hope," said Carlos ardently. "I have hope to go." He paused. "If God wants."

"Well, if you ever get the chance you really should go. New York is *muy bonita,*" she said, with a hoarse, self-conscious laugh. "There's a million things to do there."

Carlos's deep brown eyes suddenly acquired a pensive cast. With his tongue, he began to tease the inside of his mouth, under the wound. "I no go to New Yor," he said. "Never, maybe." He seemed completely bereft, as if all of life's illusions had been suddenly exposed.

"Why not?" asked Deborah.

"Because no money."

"Aah." She nodded, sighing slightly.

"I no have money, never." He got up halfway, squatting on his haunches. He looked at Deborah earnestly and began to claw at the sand by his sides. "I am working hard, I am working with my hands, *cada día, todos los días,* and I no have money. I try have money, but to eat, the medicine, the chil'rens, *la renta.*" With a quiet, extended whine, Carlos muttered a word that Peter and Deborah only recognized as an expletive. Then he beat the sand with his two sand-filled fists, an action that startled and sprayed them. Peter released a succinct snort.

Carlos smiled at him. "Hello, Meester," he said.

Peter nodded.

"You like my country?" asked Carlos.

Secretly Peter envied Deborah's social skills, and wondered what it would be like to converse genially with whoever crossed his path. But he simply couldn't. "I'm sure it's positively the most electrifying place I've ever visited," he said, lightning quick and with as much of a plum-in-his-mouth accent as he could muster. He picked up the sketch pad and pastels that had been at his side for the last hour.

Carlos didn't understand a word, but kept up his smile. He stared as Peter began to sketch a pelican hugging the shore. "You fron New Yor, too, Meester?"

"London," said Peter, staring intently at the pelican.

"London?" asked Carlos incredulously.

"Yes, London," said Peter peevishly.

Carlos let out a high-pitched shriek. "*Viva la reina!*" he screamed. The suddenness of the noise caused Peter to shudder and face Carlos, who asked him, "You know the queen?"

"I beg your pardon?"

"You know the queen?"

Not only was he dim, he was tiresome to boot, thought Peter. "No, I've never had the pleasure," he said. "Nor Fergie nor Randy Andy nor Camilla Parker-Bowles."

Carlos turned his stare toward Deborah's cascading blond curls, her red back glistening with oil and sweat, the loose pink bikini bottom, the toned expansive flesh bursting from its sides. A little white tag peered from the elastic band and cheerfully waved in the breeze. "You are very beautiful womans," he said to her.

Deborah shifted her weight on the towel and said nothing. "*Eres tan bonita que los pájaros cantan de tu belleza desde los árboles,*" continued Carlos. "*También los peces cantan cuando estás nadando.*" His words, however sweetly seductive they were meant to be, produced little effect on Deborah, who smiled uncomfortably. He turned to Peter.

"Your wife a beautiful womans," he said. Peter continued to stare at the sea, drawing furiously. Carlos got up, walked directly in front of Peter and squatted. A gray-coated tongue appeared from his mouth and he began to lap at the pulp of the red bruise. "Meester, I say you a lucky man," he said.

It crossed Peter's mind that, had he been born in this misbegotten town, by now he would have undoubtedly been obligated to prove his *machismo* by giving Carlos a second bruise on the other side of his mouth. Strangely, he found himself feeling sorry for the other man, and in his mind's eye saw himself putting a comradely arm on Carlos's shoulder. The image made him blush. "Well," he said. "I should say so. Comparatively speaking."

Carlos, licking his wound, squatted silently for a long moment. Why didn't he just go away, thought Peter. It dawned on him what he hated about this country: the threat. He had never felt so close to physical violence before. The perilous dark alleys of Brooklyn seemed like Yorkshire Dales in comparison.

Deborah tried to placate the squatting Carlos. "What's the problem?" she asked.

"Pro'lem?" he asked, still staring at Peter. "I no have pro'lem, amigo. You have pro'lem!"

"Calm down," said Deborah.

"*Tú, cálmate tú, güey!*" said Carlos bluntly to Peter. Peter noted uncomfortably that each time Deborah opened her mouth, Carlos responded to him, as if he had spoken. Therefore, he wished she'd shut up. Carlos, intensely grabbing handfuls of sand and letting them fall at his sides, said: "I no have money, *sabes*? I no go to New Yor because I no have money. You come here, to my country, to my *playa*, because you have money. *Pero te digo una cosa*, Meester—you no better than me because you have money."

"Peter, let's go," said Deborah.

"You no better than me."

"Peter, the sun's going to go down soon."

"Why don't you just go?" Peter asked Carlos sternly. "Why don't you go away and leave us alone?"

Peter watched Carlos's tight body unclench. "*Oye*, Meester," he said, looking Peter in the eye. "You fron London. I fron here, fron *los altos*." He pointed an arm to the hills beyond. "You wel-con' here. But this is *my* land." He began to stretch his arms, his hands marking lines in the sand. "This is *my playa*. You no can say to me to go away. Because this land *belong* to me." There was an uncomfortable silence. "I be your friend for all the time I can," said Carlos. "After that . . ." He shrugged. "No more words, Meester."

Peter noticed that Deborah had already folded her towel and packed away the sunscreen, her book, and Peter's pastels in her straw handbag. "Come on, Peter, let's go," she insisted hoarsely. "*Right now.*" He stood up, doubly ashamed to have been first threatened by a vagrant and then bossed around by an American harridan in an ill-fitting bikini.

"Hey," said Carlos, still staring at Peter. "Man to man. Fuck you."

They walked fifteen paces back toward their hotel when Peter suddenly became enraged. He couldn't resist a shrill rebuke, and turned toward Carlos: "You're a very disagreeable man!" he said. "We haven't done a thing to you! You should learn to leave others in peace!"

Carlos howled, literally. "*Ándale, anímate, cabrón!*" he shouted. "*Órale!*" Laughing, he grabbed handfuls of sand and threw them in Peter and Deborah's direction. There weren't many people around to look, but had there been a handy hole in the ground, Peter would have crawled into it.

Peter thought he knew what it was like to be poor. When he was thirteen, his father had lost a fortune in what he called bad investments, the majority of which had been made in gambling clubs and betting shops. The family had to move from a large house in Hampstead to a smaller one in Pimlico, where Peter shared a room with his younger brother, a fact he didn't dare impart to his classmates at St. Paul's, who he imagined all had their own spacious rooms, as he'd had before.

Creditors wrote polite letters, then phoned, then came to the door but were ignored at every turn. Finally his father disappeared (only to resurface a year later living with a wealthy widow in Malta). His mother actually went to work (unprecedented in her family), opening a decorating business. Peter's maternal grandparents began to contribute to the family's support.

They still sent Peter money, but on his thirtieth birthday suggested it was time he consider finding a suitable profession. Peter was immensely offended; their thousand-dollar monthly stipend was hardly enough to support him in New York in the first place. He already supplemented his allowance with surges of work, usually assisting painters—stretching their canvases, running errands to art supply stores, cleaning the dishes from which they ate lunch. They paid him pitiful wages; his revenge lay in performing his tasks with aggressive lethargy.

But here on holiday in a hellish place he was discovering a poverty that he had known existed in theory but never actually seen in evidence. In misbegotten Mexico, you couldn't escape it. Not even in the supposedly safe haven of the expensive restaurant on whose veranda he and Deborah were dining. Overlooking the sea and the embankment, amid a handful of nattering American tourists, obsequious waiters, and roving guitarists, Peter was constantly interrupted with pesky reminders of the sordid lives of the locals.

For instance, in the middle of their dinner, a silent vendor in indigenous dress appeared, trying to sell embroidered bracelets for pennies. After Deborah had said, *"No, gracias,"* the woman just stood there with an imploring look on her face. Finally, to get rid of her, Peter reached in his pocket and gave her a coin. She examined its denomination, muttered a contemptuous exclamation, and threw it on the ground. A complete nutter! She probably had far more money than he did, stashed under a straw mattress in her hut, or teepee, or wherever it was that she lived. From here on, he would trust his original instinct to resolutely ignore all beggars.

Not without his sentimental side, Peter found it harder to resist the skinny cat who rubbed its body against his legs, mewling for a table scrap. He fed it a fat piece of shrimp. A dinner, composed of six of them and a greasy clump of white rice, cost fifteen dollars, a price that would unquestionably be paid by Deborah.

Peter assumed that her offer to buy him an airline ticket after he claimed penury meant that she would cover every expense. Only after her distasteful coaxing would he agree to part with a peso for his share of a meal, a hotel room, even a coffee. He had a way of blankly staring into space each time a check arrived, a state of unconsciousness he could maintain for an indefinite period of time. On the occasions when she asked him for money point-blank, he made a great fuss of taking out a weathered leather change purse and painstakingly extracting coins and bills of small denomination. It was then difficult for him to actually let go of them, as if they'd been glued to his fingertips. Finally he would make a fuss about not understanding the rate of exchange, and evoke pounds sterling despite having lived in New York for two years. "Maths have never been my forte," he'd curtly explain.

It had been impulsive of Deborah to invite Peter on holiday with her in the first place. She'd asked him a month earlier, the day after they'd met at a crowded and noisy loft party under the Brooklyn side of the Manhattan Bridge. Flushed with red wine, she had been entertained by his unrelenting negative pronounce-ments against New York: its absurdly frenetic pace, the "nutters" rollerblading down Broadway at two in the morning, the oily tri-angles of pizza that, to so many residents, passed for a proper meal.

His contrary nature and schoolmarmish tone amused her, and she was also attracted to his lean, willowy frame. In strange contrast to his awkwardness were the elegant gestures he made with his long fingers. She wondered what it might feel like to have them fluttering along her body. At two in the morning, she urged him to her apartment in Murray Hill, where they made polite small talk over a shared bottle of beer until he let her push him on the bed, and kiss him, her hard teeth pressing into his lips, the expanse of her flushed torso enveloping his lanky limbs. He was so passive that she hardly felt those long fingers at all; nonetheless, she was excited by playing the aggressor for a change.

At the party, he told her he'd be returning to England in a month. Over coffee the following morning, she impetuously sug-gested he come along on this trip she'd already planned, imagining the vacation as his last fling before returning to the Old World. When he protested that he had little money, she offered to pay his airfare. The price of the discounted flight meant nothing to her; she had a well-paying job as an editor in the publications wing of a brokerage house. After objecting showily, Peter accepted.

But as the two weeks before the vacation passed, it surfaced that the date of Peter's return to England was extremely flexible. He didn't even have a ticket home. And he'd pointedly mentioned several times that the people at whose Brooklyn loft the party had been held were now getting tired of his sleeping on a foam mattress in their kitchen, an arrangement they had endured for the past three months. He was now spending several nights a week at her apartment, and had grown neither more amiable nor more amorous than he'd been the night they met.

"Good God," Peter said, staring into the distance. "Isn't that the nutter from the beach this afternoon?"

Deborah looked up; indeed there was Carlos standing on the embankment with his chin at his chest, receiving what seemed to be a rebuke from a khaki-clad policeman with a pot belly. "That's him," she said.

"Rotten luck to have been nabbed by a bandito," said Peter with a titter. "Well, let them sort it out among themselves, they're all mad here."

Deborah paused pensively. "I have to admit," she said, "that what he said got to me. About not having any money."

"You're joking," said Peter, his voice rising to a near screech.

"It made me feel bad," she said. She glanced over at Carlos, his head now held high, talking animatedly. The cop stroked his thick black mustache while he listened. "You know, that we can travel and he can't. He's probably never been out of Puerto de los Santos."

"Don't be so gullible, Deborah," snorted Peter. "His poor children and all that. If he didn't spend his money on drink, he could take all the trips to New York he wanted." Was it Peter's imagination, or were Carlos and the bandito looking over at him and Deborah? He thought they were, albeit discreetly.

"Peter, you're crazy." She said it with a smile, but her throaty voice was cracking. "The minimum wage here is three dollars a day. If you earned three dollars a day, you'd drink too."

"He's looking at us, you know. I don't earn very much money, either, Deborah, but I don't spend all day crying about it and blaming the rest of the world."

"You can't compare what you earn and what they earn." Deborah sighed loudly. "He's not looking at us at all."

"Well, he was before. And I can, in a way. Here everyone lives on fish and coconuts and is presumably wildly happy because they don't know any better. They have the sun, they have the sea, what else do they need? Life is actually much harder in New York."

"Peter," she said, "he probably lives in a hut with a straw roof! Three dollars a day, on some, I don't know, construction crew, or chain gang. Like a convict! Like a slave! Have you ever seen Sebastiao Salgado's pictures? They work really hard here."

"Our little friend didn't seem to be working very hard this afternoon," said Peter, chortling. "All I saw him do was sit on the beach, reeking of the rum he'd drunk all morning. Or all week." Now Carlos and the potbellied cop were laughing together. The cop slapped Carlos's back and stomped the ground with his black boot; Carlos nodded his head eagerly.

A sad-faced boy with heavy-lidded ebony eyes, about eight or nine years old, began to tug at Peter's sleeve, mumbling in a musical whisper. Peter laughed. "Another nutter, junior division. I see they let him off the chain gang early today." The boy, speaking without interruption, was making gestures toward the seat where Deborah had left her straw handbag and Peter his sketchbook.

"*Qué querer?*" asked Deborah, looking at the boy.

"Go away," said Peter quickly and deliberately. "We've finished our food and we don't have any money." The boy kept talking.

The meaning of a word the boy said, *dibujar,* somehow found its way into Deborah's brain, although she hadn't used it since her high school Spanish classes. "He wants to draw a picture," said Deborah. "He wants to use your sketchbook and pastels."

"Tell him to buy his own."

"Peter!" she said hoarsely. "He's a little boy. Give him a break."

"Oh, all right." Peter sighed. "I may as well inaugurate the Puerto de los Santos School of Fine Arts."

"Go ahead," said Deborah to the boy, removing her purse from the chair and gesturing to the boy. "*Dibujar.*"

The boy, now smiling, sat in the chair and began to compose a detailed sketch of the seascape. He resisted Deborah's attempts at conversation, preferring to draw in silence. As a slender waiter in a guayabera cleared their dinner plates, Deborah ordered a tea for herself and an orange juice for the boy. Peter asked for another rum and tonic. As the boy drew, they sat in silence, serenely watching the ocean, as if they were a small family.

When he finished the drawing, the boy showed Deborah the result. For a child, it was remarkably sophisticated, rendering the movement of the waves, the moonlight on the water.

"*Qué bonita,*" she said. "*Muy bueno.*"

The boy, arms outstretched, drawing in hand, mumbled something to Deborah, imploring with his eyes. "What?" she asked. "You want me to have it?"

"He probably wants to sell it to you. An industrious lad," said Peter.

"No," said Deborah, smiling at the boy. "I can't take it. Why don't you take it home to your mother?"

The boy, babbling musically, put the drawing on Deborah's lap.

"Deborah, you are about to become the child's de Medici," said Peter. "Ask him how much he wants. Let the negotiations begin."

The slender waiter appeared. "He want you to have it, *señorita*," he said to Deborah. "He want to give it to you."

"Thank you, you're so sweet," she said to the boy, caressing his cheek. "But don't you want to keep it? Don't you want to hang it on your wall?"

The waiter said something to the boy, who answered him back quickly. The waiter laughed, and then translated for Deborah. "He say he don't need the picture because he already have the ocean."

A warm breeze, the light of the moon, and the sound of the charging waves filtered through the venetian blinds of Deborah and Peter's hotel room. He lay on his back staring at the still ceiling fan. She sat looking toward the window, leaning against the bed's carved wooden headboard. They were naked.

"Sorry," he muttered.

"Don't worry," she said. "A lot of men feel that condoms are not exactly conducive—"

"Yes, well," he interrupted. "There are . . . complications . . . at the moment . . ."

"Don't worry," she said. After some discreet hesitation, she asked, "Do you want to talk about it?"

"Well, I'm not sure that there's terribly much to talk about," he sputtered, covering the lower half of his body with the sheet. "When I get back to New York I'm going to have to find another place to live. I have no idea where. It's a terrible bore."

"Terrible," Deborah said, barely suppressing a smile.

"I mean, this happens from time to time. I'm certain I won't end up one of your famous homeless, sleeping in a giant cardboard box atop a subway grating."

"Oh, I'm sure you won't."

"It's just a bother. Sometimes I'd like to have a more settled existence."

She smiled quizzically, but with sympathy. "You would?" she asked.

"Yes," he said. "But I may indeed have to go back to London to get it."

"That's great," she said with, by Peter's estimation, a jot too much enthusiasm. "I mean, weren't you going to go back anyway?"

"Well, yes," he said. "Eventually. I just wasn't sure when."

"Maybe you should go sooner rather than later," she said. "Let's face it, you've never really liked New York, did you? You're always complaining about it."

"No, I like New York. Except that it's such a hard place. The people are so hard. They think of nothing but money, never of life."

She stroked his fine black hair. "It's softer in London," she said.

Cunt, he thought. What did she know about it, anyway? "Well, people in London think about more than money, and their jobs," he said. "I mean, you can actually have a coherent conversation about something besides how much rent you pay and what position you've most recently been promoted to." He thought about the patronizing half smiles of his teachers at Chelsea College of Art, the pennies he had earned as a freelance subeditor at an art magazine.

"I'm sure you'll be much happier there," said Deborah.

"You're probably right." Why did Americans go on about happiness so ponderously? He looked at her heavy breasts with their large brownish aureoles, and felt disgust.

Sudden, staccato raps at the door made them both jump. The

door opened, and the overhead light flashed on. Deborah grabbed a towel from the back of a chair and did the best she could to cover herself.

Four khaki-clad policemen entered the room. The last one, his gun drawn, slammed the door shut. In his late thirties, he was the oldest of the group by far. He had a pot belly and a thick mustache.

"I say," said Peter. "I think you chaps have the wrong room."

The potbellied cop stood in front of the bed, looking at Peter and Deborah with a paternal smile. He put his gun back in its holster. Two of his youthful cohorts began to handle postcards, a bottle of suntan lotion, articles of clothing that had been left on top of the table, splayed across the chairs, scattered on the dresser. The fourth cop went to the window and looked outside through the slats of the blinds. Deborah watched the drawing of the seascape that the child had given her sail to the floor.

Slowly and calmly, the potbellied cop spoke to Peter and Deborah. His manner bespoke kindness, experience, good humor. Peter could understand a few words: . . . *problema . . . formal . . . pasaporte . . .*

"Let me handle this, Peter," said Deborah in a quavering voice. "Just stay calm." And then to the cop: "*Usted . . . querer . . .* passport?"

"*Sí, señorita,*" he said. "*Exactamente.*"

"We have money," she said. "*Dinero.*"

"Don't give them any money," said Peter crossly.

"Peter," she said gravely, "I said let me handle this."

"Money, money, money," said one of the others, a youth with a thin whisper of a mustache. He held Deborah's black brassiere in his hand, and said something with a grin on his face.

"*Con cuidado,*" said the potbellied one.

"*No problemo,*" she said. She arranged the towel, got out of bed, and walked over to her nylon carry-on bag. As she kneeled to unzip its inside pocket, where she kept documents and money, her pink ripened-mango buttocks emerged from under the towel. Peter could feel the temperature rise in the room. The youth next to the window closed the venetian blinds.

"Take it," said Deborah, smiling through her terror, suspending the towel in front of her breasts with one hand and offering her passport and a wad of money with the other. "You can have it all."

The potbellied cop took what was proffered, looked it over absently, and put it in his pocket. He returned Deborah's smile with what looked to Peter like gratitude. As he began to speak again, his expression became increasingly grave. "*Delincuente . . . federales . . . narcotraficantes . . .*"

Suddenly, with the back of his hand, he slapped her across the face. There was an enormous crack, her towel dropped, and she fell, gasping, across the bed. The youth with the sparse mustache yanked Peter out of bed by a bony arm. Dreadfully frightened, Peter covered his sex with his other hand until he was shocked to feel the young cop's foot smash into his narrow behind. He fell in a heap in front of the closet. The young cop, pointing his pistol, in sharp guttural words ordered Peter inside. He sat on the floor, his head among the dangling trousers suspended from hangers. The cop grabbed Peter's hair and pushed his face to the floor.

"Ouch," he said. Quelling his terror and humiliation, Peter thought, *If only I could somehow find a way through the door.* Then he felt the cold metal of the pistol's barrel against his cheekbone, and moved his eyes toward the savage expression on the young cop's face.

The boy, still holding Deborah's bra with his other hand, moved the pistol from Peter's cheek and watched his three cohorts beat her ruthlessly. They dealt blow after blow across her face, her breasts, her back, her round buttocks. She didn't make a sound, not even a whimper. From the floor of the closet, Peter could see part of the bed and the spectacular beating. The older cop unzipped his pants and began to rub his penis. Peter imagined that Deborah's pain was so intense that when they got around to raping her, it would come as a relief. It will soon be over, he told himself.

Blood trickled from Deborah's mouth. Her stomach rose and fell with each heavy breath. A bad lot, thought Peter. Again and again, he repeated to himself that it would soon be over, and that all they wanted was their money and Deborah's body, in its blond, viscous, overripe glory. He had been right all along about Mexico, but what a beastly way to have one's point proven. He wondered if they wouldn't have been better off if she'd refrained from prancing around Puerto de los Santos in her bikini before the banditos.

It will soon be over, he heard himself say yet again. His eyes moved from the floor, where the drawing of the sea was now smudged with the policemen's boot prints, to one of the boy cops, also unzipping his pants and rubbing himself. Peter felt a stirring in his own groin. This hadn't happened involuntarily in years. He folded his knees to his chest.

La Quedada

i couldn't believe the dress," said Sarita Liebkind, shaking her head. "The train must have been ten meters long. Ruth may have lost a little weight, but the way the skirt puffed out didn't exactly show off her new figure."

"What new figure?" asked Jessica Finkelstein. "She lost two kilos. Ruth has the biggest ass in Mexico City. She needed all that skirt to cover it."

"She looked more like a wedding cake than a bride," said Sarita. "Her father must have paid a fortune for it."

Jessica, pausing for effect, dragged on her cigarette. "Three thousand dollars," she said, smoke emanating from her bulbous nose and carmine-painted mouth. "It's a Bob Mackie."

"*No me digas,*" said Sarita, her pale face flushing almost to the brilliant natural red of her hair. "That's like, what?" She tried to calculate in her head. "More than two hundred thousand pesos." She shook a Marlboro Light from her soft pack, and helped herself to Jessica's plastic lighter. She had long fingers, with nails bitten to the quick.

"The dress is the least of it," said Jessica, running a hand through her thick mane, which had been dyed from dark brown to auburn. "Those flowers!" Sarita and Jessica giggled, remembering the ridiculous centerpieces of gardenias, orchids, and tiger lilies that snaked up in four-foot-tall arrangements at each table at the wedding banquet. They had made it impossible to see anyone sitting across from you.

"The two bands, and the string quartet during the ceremony," said Sarita.

"Food and drink for five hundred people at the Camino Real," Jessica continued, counting on her fingers. Fouquet's de Paris, the hotel's most expensive restaurant, had catered the affair under the supervision of a rabbi. The scotch had been Chivas Regal, the vodka Absolut. The dinner consisted of smoked salmon, wild mushroom soup, and steak *au poivre,* accompanied by wines imported from France. If he could have, Ruth's father would have served shrimp and *langostinos,* which were even more extravagantly expensive. But shellfish were prohibited. Notwithstanding what they might have eaten at home or in restaurants, all weddings in the Jewish community were kosher.

"Then he's sending them on their honeymoon," Jessica added. "Four nights at Las Brisas and three weeks in Europe."

"How much do you think he paid for everything?" asked Sarita. "The grand total."

"I don't know," said Jessica, shrugging. "Fifty thousand dollars? A hundred thousand dollars?"

"*Más café?*" The waitress, brown-skinned, in a pink polyester uniform, stood before their table, a coffee pot in her hand. Sarita noted with chagrin that whenever she or her friends mentioned some outrageous quantity of money, out of the blue appeared a dying-of-hunger waitress, maid, shoeshine boy, or lottery ticket vendor. No wonder everyone thought all Mexican Jews were rich.

"*Sí, por favor,*" said Sarita.

As she poured the coffee, the waitress noticed that the girl with the freckles and red hair had hardly touched her *enchiladas suizas,* while the other *güera,* with the dyed hair and big nose, had eaten maybe half of her *carne tampiqueña.* Before, they'd had maybe three spoonfuls of soup each. And they were already smoking their postprandial cigarettes. It was one of life's paradoxes that people with money could afford not to eat. "*Ya terminaron?*" she asked.

"*Sí,*" said Sarita flatly. She couldn't eat much; she was developing an ulcer. Jessica nodded her head, thinking of her figure. The waitress cleared the plates.

"I would never have a wedding like that," said Sarita. "If it was me, I'd rather spend less getting married and keep the money to start out. Put a down payment on an apartment."

"What down payment? He bought them an apartment, too. Three bedrooms in Tecamachalco," said Jessica. "It doesn't make any difference to Ruth's father. He wipes his ass with bills! He has to pay people to think up ways to spend it."

Sarita shook her head. Other people's wealth stung her. There was no justice to it. Since her father had run off with his secretary to Cabo San Lucas five years earlier, Sarita's family had been living off the largesse of her mother's brothers. They didn't lack for anything, but were on a strict budget, at least compared to her friends. And her guilt-stricken mother always anguished about money. The precariousness, the helplessness, the panic, made Sarita miserable.

"And I suppose he's giving Alex a job, too?" Sarita referred to the man who had been Ruth's husband for the past twenty-four hours.

"Of course," said Jessica. "He'll give Alex some office with a phone and a desk he can put his feet on. But it's just so Ruth's father will know where he is during the day."

"What a son of a bitch," said Sarita, who, unlike most of her friends, actually had to work to earn her own pocket money, as an executive secretary to an organization that raised funds for Israel. "You know Alex used to beat Karen." She referred to Alex's first wife, whom he had divorced a year earlier, at the age of twenty-five.

"Beat her, cheated on her, took money from her," said Jessica. "You name it."

Sarita voiced a longtime suspicion. "I always thought he was a *puto.*"

"I'm going to tell you something," said Jessica, her nostrils flaring. "You know why they got divorced?"

"Because he was a good-for-nothing son of a bitch," said Sarita passionately, thinking of Alex's blond hair, pale blue eyes, and golden smile. He had looked beautiful beside Ruth in his double-breasted tuxedo. "He beat her. He gave her a black eye. Remember when Karen came to the *deportivo* and swam in the pool wearing those ridiculous brown sunglasses? 'I opened the freezer door and it smashed me in the eye.' Did she think anyone would believe a *bobe meisa* like that?"

Jessica shook her head. "That she could live with."

"What do you mean?"

"I mean that beating Karen was bad, but that was between the two of them. What broke the camel's back was when she came home one day and found him in bed with another man."

Sarita, coughing wildly, practically choked on her cigarette smoke. "I knew it," she said in a strangled voice. "Who?"

Jessica shrugged. "I don't know. Some goy," she said with a shudder.

Sarita swallowed a mouthful of coffee, but it didn't alleviate the bad taste. "Why would Ruth's parents let her marry a shmuck like Alex?" she asked. "Everyone knows how he treated Karen."

"I guess they'd prefer their daughter to be unhappily married than to be *una quedada*," said Jessica, and immediately wished she hadn't. Sarita, at twenty-nine and without prospects for a husband, was well on her way to being left behind, to *quedada*-hood.

They sat in silence for a few minutes, finishing their cigarettes and coffee. Finally Sarita blurted out what she'd wished to say all evening. "Just promise me you won't have a wedding like that."

Jessica rubbed her plump nose self-consciously and looked intently at the ashtray as she stubbed out her cigarette. Things had certainly become strained between the two friends since Jessica and Jacobo, Sarita's brother, had announced their engagement. The two women saw each other much less frequently than they had before, and Jacobo made matters worse by insisting to Jessica that he didn't like his sister to be the third wheel on their dates.

"In the end that's really up to my parents," Jessica said. "I'm starting to see their side of it. Look, I'm their only daughter. If it gives them *naches* to spend their money, who am I to tell them not to?"

These words were like a knife in Sarita's heart. If it made her miserable to be still unmarried, she'd at least had the contentment of silently sharing her agony with Jessica, who, despite her family's wealth, had until recently threatened to become one of the Jewish community's most conspicuous *quedadas*. Six months ago Jacobo and Jessica, with their announcement, had pulled the rug out from under Sarita.

Sarita could picture the wedding they would have—Jessica's father would see to it that the event was, if possible, even gaudier than Ruth and Alex's. There would be a ridiculously exorbitant menu, and two dance bands that would play until four in the morning, when the mariachis would arrive and breakfast would be served. Five hundred guests would gossip that Jacobo was marrying

Jessica for her father's money (a suspicion Sarita shared). Jessica would look, if not as fat, then surely as ridiculous as Ruth had, in a wedding-cake dress out of *Bride's* magazine.

Sarita felt utterly alone. She decided that, in the last analysis, Jessica wasn't any different from the rest of the girls in the community. She was just another JAP. In such an instance, the acronym stood for Jewish Aztec Princess.

"You still haven't explained the difference between the chip that Ichikawa's developing and the one that Fujimora's already selling." Aarón spoke in flawless English through the cellular phone. He plugged his other ear with a finger, so he could hear his man in Tokyo through the din of the technopop mixes that infused the Bar Mata. It was midnight in Mexico City; the Nikkei would close in a couple of hours. "Then I'll ask you again: why is twenty-one a good price?"

Sarita sipped her Absolut and tonic slowly. It was a bit embarrassing to be sitting in a bar with a man blabbing intently on his cellular, but she indulged Aarón because they were old friends. They'd gone to school together as children, and five years earlier he'd pursued her like a bloodhound. She confessed that although she cherished his friendship she wasn't romantically inclined toward him, and somehow their relationship had withstood the blow.

"I'm not convinced," he said. "The dollar's up against the yen." These were still his business hours. Aarón had made a fortune selling the peso short just before the devaluation three years earlier. Overnight he'd metamorphosed from a nerd shlepping his narrow ass around a brokerage house to an authoritative financial guru, now building his second bundle administrating a hedge fund for a consortium of wealthy Mexicans. He'd also become one of the most sought-after bachelors in the Jewish community, dating many of its daughters.

Biting her nails, Sarita looked around the dark, cavernous bar, with its track lighting and industrial gray tables and chairs. Bar Mata was packed, with two hundred or so twenty-somethings, the boys wearing double-breasted suits and mousse in their hair, the girls in minidresses or long skirts with their midriffs exposed. Each cocktail cost twice what a Mexican laborer earned in a day. She had been here ten days earlier, on a blind date with a young Jewish man from Monterrey. They had been set up by one of Sarita's cousins. Her swain had been the only hunchback under thirty Sarita had ever seen. The thought of him gave her gastric pains.

"Look, I already got burned on technology stocks in the States. It's not going to happen twice," said Aarón, adjusting his gold-framed glasses, which had slipped down his nose. "If it goes down to eighteen before the close, I'll buy; otherwise, fuck it." Aarón folded the phone and placed it in a holster in his belt. "I'm sorry," he said, switching to Spanish with a self-deprecating smile. "It's ridiculous for me to do that in here. But it could be an important trade."

"Don't worry," said Sarita. "It's your job."

Neither money nor position made him any more attractive. He was short, slight, even scrawny, and at thirty-one half-bald. He grew his hair long on the sides and teased it in several directions to cover his scalp. He insisted on wearing Italian suits with shoulders so padded they made his head look tiny. Nonetheless, his success with other women was beginning to make Sarita feel more single, more alone. More *quedada*.

"You know, Aarón," she said, "I envy you. I wish I had work that I enjoyed."

"It's not as marvelous as it looks," he answered, draining his

Chivas and signaling the waiter for another. "I'm up all night. I can never get away for very long. I bring my cellular phone and laptop with me even when I go away for the weekend." He raised an eyebrow suggestively. "I won't go into details, but sometimes a call will come at the least opportune moment." He laughed wryly. "Do you know how much my phone bill was last month? Four thousand dollars."

Sure enough, the waiter appeared at that very moment. "Another Chivas, *caballero*?" he asked Aarón. He was dark-skinned, with a ponytail and a lithe narrow body under his tight white shirt.

"Yes, please," said Aarón. "Are you okay or do you want another?" he asked Sarita. The waiter looked at her, with an attractively expectant expression.

"No, I'm still drinking this one," Sarita said.

"Bring her another one," Aarón said, laughing conspiratorially toward the waiter.

Another song, which had ten years earlier sounded treacly but had now been thrust through the remix recycler with a relentless percussive beat, pulsated through the bar.

Aarón pushed his gold-framed glasses up his nose, a grim smile on his face. "I went to Zihuatanejo last month, for a weekend," he said. "I didn't even tell anyone I was going. I was all by myself. No phone, no computer, no Yemile." The latter was a wealthy Jewess of Syrian descent whom he'd been squiring in recent months, who wore a perpetually displeased expression known as a *cara de hígado encebollado*—a liver-and-onions face. Sighing deeply, he said, "It was such a *hueva* to come back."

His bitterness registered, but Sarita didn't know what to make of it. "Real life is always disappointing after a vacation," she said. "That's an inescapable fact."

He looked up at the ceiling. "I wonder if the fact is that real life is disappointing, period," he said.

"What are you talking about?" she asked.

Aarón looked at her, rubbing his lips with his thumb and forefinger. "Did you ever want to just say fuck you to everyone?" Now he was looking into her eyes, with an expression that combined aggression and amusement. "I mean, did you ever feel like you were living a life that had been preordained for you by other forces? Like there's this supernatural power making you do things that aren't really what you want to do?"

"Well, sort of," she said.

"I'd like to go away and never come back," he said. "Open a bar. Like this . . . no, not like this. Quieter. Without the shitty music. On the beach somewhere. On an island. Romantic, under a big *palapa,* with candles. Have you ever been to La Casa que Canta in Zihuatanejo?"

"So why don't you?" she asked. "If that's what you want, do it. You've got enough money. Isn't that the whole point of making money? So you can do what you want?" At that moment, more strongly than ever, Sarita yearned to be rich.

Aarón ran scrawny fingers across the top of his head, checking that his hair had stayed in place. "You know why I don't?" he said. "Because I'm afraid I'll find out, after a couple of years, that I want to come back."

"So then come back! That's no reason not to go in the first place! My God, Aarón, you're only thirty! You don't have to have your whole entire life planned out until you drop dead."

He wore an expression of pure resignation. "My parents are here. Yemile is here. You're here. Everyone I know is here."

Sarita sighed. She wanted to say, *Fuck them. All of them.* But Aarón abruptly interrupted her train of thought. "Did you ever want to go to bed with a goy?" he asked.

At which moment the good-looking waiter appeared. He was smiling; Sarita wondered if he even knew what the word *goy* meant. She smiled back at him. "Another whiskey for you, *caballero,* and an Absolut and tonic for you," he said.

"*Gracias,*" she said. Aarón suddenly seemed feeble to her: there weren't any twilight-zone flying saucers making him do things he didn't want to do. She thought of her anguished mother, her aunts and uncles, her brother and sister, everyone in the community really, who with each look, gesture, and word, seemed to be appraising, assessing, judging her with disapproval, asking *When will you finally unearth a nice Jewish man?* Sarita imagined that Aarón's obnoxious family was in the driver's seat, pressuring him, but in the end, he was the only one responsible for his unhappiness.

She considered answering his question about wanting to have sex with *goyim* truthfully, even if he would be shocked. She had, in fact, had a few encounters with non-Jewish males, whom she'd met at parties, and one whom she'd let pick her up at a restaurant. She wasn't *marrying* them, after all, and she'd been impeccably discreet; if she'd been found out she'd have created a scandal in the cloistered Jewish community. Because of this, she reconsidered answering Aarón. Anything was fair game for gossip; whatever she told him would likely be distributed like a news flash from Polanco to Lomas the following morning. "The thought has crossed my mind," she said cautiously, and then regretted having even gone that far. She bit her thumbnail.

Perhaps Aarón didn't hear her; in any event, he kept talking. "There's this woman at the *casa de bolsa* where I worked. An exceptional stockbroker. Tall, gorgeous, smart; she made shitloads of money. We could really talk. We got along so well." He drank half his scotch in one gulp. "But not only was she a goy, she was a *morenita.* From Veracruz. As dark as—" He looked around, and pointed: "The waiter," he said. "Imagine me bringing her home to meet my parents! They'd disown me. They'd throw me out of the house and never speak to me again." He laughed bitterly, removing his glasses and rubbing his eyes.

"So, you mean, you had to cut it off with her?"

"Cut what off?" he asked. "I never even asked her out."

Sarita sighed. His hopelessness made her angry, so she took the plunge. "Aarón," she said. "I actually had an affair with a Gentile. Once."

"Good for you," he said, smiling, clearly impressed. "You have more guts than I do. *Salud.*" He lifted his glass and drank from it. "Who was he?"

"You don't know him," she said. "I met him at a party, at a friend of a friend's in San Jerónimo." The memory of Gerardo, wide-eyed, slender, and attractive, in a soft, wine-colored shirt, burnished by the three vodka and tonics Sarita had consumed, made her smile fondly.

"How did it happen? What did he say?"

"Well, not that much." She laughed. "We were dancing, mostly. You know how when it gets really late at a party someone always puts on slow music?" The memory became more vivid to her; despite her surroundings, she could practically feel Gerardo's arms around her, hear his whisper in her ear. "He told me that ever since he'd been thirteen years old he'd dreamed of making love to a redhead." She laughed and then blushed.

Aarón had had similar fantasies about redheads for a commensurate period of time. "Did he know you were Jewish?"

Sarita looked at Aarón looking at her, at the desire in his eyes, and fleetingly felt ravishing. "Sure," she said. "I told him."

"And what did he say?"

She leaned in, as if to exchange an intimacy. "He asked if anyone in my family had personally killed Christ. And if we drank the blood of Catholic babies at holidays."

Aarón fumbled with his cigarettes. "That's what they all think of us," he said.

"Not him," said Sarita, remembering Gerardo's tight body in her arms. "All he wanted was to sleep with the enemy."

Aarón smiled, and then looked at her with resolve. "Do you know what I'd really like to do?"

"What?"

"Go to a hotel. Now. With you."

"Excuse me?"

"Let's go to a hotel," he said. "Let's make love!"

"No!" she said.

"Come on! We're old friends! You know I've always been crazy about you." He laid a bony-fingered hand atop hers.

"No, Aarón," she said firmly. "Listen, I think it's time to go home. You've had too much to drink."

"I'm not drunk," he said. "Okay, I am. A little. But my mind has never been clearer. I know exactly what I'm saying. I want to make love to you. Do you know that you're more beautiful than ever? You're one of those girls that gets more exquisite as she gets older."

She was not immune to flattery. "Come on, Aarón," she said. "Enough."

"Let's just do it. Let's be happy." His hand snaked up her arm, covered in a gauzy green blouse. "Let's forget everything else and allow ourselves an hour—no, two hours!—of pure love and pleasure! Without worrying about anything else. Or anyone. Or what people will say. This is what I really want to do." He leaned in to kiss her on the neck, and tottered as Sarita shifted in her seat.

"You're being very obnoxious," Sarita said, helping to steady him. She considered him without his glasses and wondered if perhaps he wasn't quite so ugly. Last Saturday at lunch one of her uncles had suggested that it was perhaps because her standards were too high that she didn't have a boyfriend. She'd dismissed him at once but secretly wondered if she shouldn't be more willing to focus on a man's appealing qualities. "If we go to bed together," she said, "we'll ruin our friendship."

"No, we won't," said Aarón, his voice intensifying. "We'll just take it to a higher level."

He wasn't a bad person; he was just sort of geeky-looking. But he was nice, and she'd suspected all along that he was still in love with her. Could you grow to love someone, because he loved you?

And she couldn't deny that he was wealthy. She imagined herself preparing dinner in a house in Tecamachalco, their three children waiting for him to come home. Then she pictured his alternate dream: holding hands on the shore of Zihuatanejo at sunset. Neither fantasy precisely left her trembling with anticipation, but nor did the idea of living in her mother's house everlastingly, suffering her family's harsh judgments. In her mind's eye, she imagined Jessica walking down the aisle with her brother, and that settled it.

He was a better lover than she'd anticipated: slow and relaxed, but passionate, and almost maddeningly attentive. It was good to know there wouldn't be a problem in bed. And he wasn't a cheapskate, either—he'd taken her to a modern, discreet hotel on a quiet side street a few blocks from the Zona Rosa for their tryst, and not some fleabag. Well, he was rich enough to make the Four Seasons his *hotel de paso*.

In the soft light of a lamp by the desk, Aarón foraged in the minibar. "There's no Absolut. But there's Vodka Wyborowa."

"Thanks," she said. "I don't want anything. Just a cigarette."

A whiskey and soda in his hand, he crossed the room back to

the bed, slowly, confidently. He looked better naked than dressed, thought Sarita: more wiry than skinny, and muscular. He kept in shape. If only she could convince him to wear clothes that were more suitable for his body.

Aarón lit both cigarettes in his mouth at the same time, and passed her one. "There," he said, and caressed her soft face with two fingers. "That wasn't so bad, was it?"

"You know it wasn't," she said. The cigarette still in her mouth, she clasped her hands behind her neck, and watched him watch her breasts lift.

He brushed one softly with the back of his hand. "You see what I was saying? Our friendship is far from ruined," he said, his eyebrows lowered.

"Come here," she said.

He climbed back into bed. "As far as I'm concerned," he said, "this is just the start of something much more meaningful."

She allowed herself to think that maybe he was right, that maybe she wouldn't end her days alone, that maybe the tortoise sometimes wins the race. She put her arms around him and kissed him, and then his cellular phone rang. He looked at his watch and then got up to answer it. "Hello," he said, and turned around, facing the window.

Sarita watched him. "Nothing, working, what about you? What are you doing, calling at this hour?" he said. His voice was slightly aloof, distant. "No, no, no, but I might be getting an important call from Japan." He looked at Sarita briefly, then out the window again. "Yes, tomorrow of course. At two o'clock sharp. No, I won't be late." There was an uncomfortable pause. "I love you, too," he said finally, and sighed. "Until tomorrow." He clicked off his phone and put it on the table.

Sarita stared at him. Aarón smiled with the expression of a man trying to remember a phrase in a foreign language that refused to flow past the tip of his tongue. Finally, he exhaled briefly and effortfully. "By the way, darling," he said to her. "Don't do anything on March twenty-third. You're invited to a wedding."

She looked at the lamp by the bed, and considered picking it up and throwing it at him. "Whose?" she asked sternly.

"Mine. And Yemile's."

She wanted to make sure she understood the story before she disemboweled him. "You mean you asked me to come here with you and deliberately waited until we went to bed before telling me you're going to marry Yemile?"

"No, no," he said, sitting in the love seat across the room. "It's a funny thing. Once you've set a wedding date, you forget that you're the only one that knows it. Do you know what I mean?" He laughed, the smoke emanating from his mouth and nostrils. "No, I guess you wouldn't. In any case, the invitations are going out this weekend."

After discovering that the lamp was in fact affixed to the bedside table, Sarita got up and began to dress herself as quickly as possible. "Don't be like that," he said. "You should congratulate me."

"I should cut your prick off," she said.

"Oh, come on." He laughed. "We can still, you know, see each other."

"Is that what you think?" she said, fuming. "You stupid, lying shit. You shameless bastard."

He laughed again. "Please don't be angry," he said. "I'm sorry. It was a mistake, but I couldn't resist you. You know I love you."

"And I hate you! I hate you because you're a liar!"

"What do you mean? I didn't lie about anything!"

"Yes, you did! You know I would have never gone to bed with you if I knew you were getting married!"

He laughed even harder. "But I didn't lie! I never said I *wasn't* getting married!" She had never dressed so quickly in her life. She turned to the door. "Wait a minute," he said. "Don't take it so hard! Wait!"

She looked at him witheringly. "Is there anything else you want?"

"Look," he said, "I say this as a friend. Did it ever occur to you that you're such a *quedada* because you take yourself so seriously? Don't go, Sarita!" he said. "Let me drive you home."

"I'll get a cab," she said and walked out, slamming the door behind her.

REGRETS

*f*ernando Fulgor, Fefu to his fans, Ferrus to his friends, leans against a brick backdrop painted a bleeding, glossy red, wearing the same salacious smile that, since he became famous at the preposterously early age of twelve, has turned millions of palpitating teenaged girls into canned heat.

The smile is directed conspiratorially at me. Dozens of bodies fill the studio—the director, the director of photography, the art director; the producer, the executive producer, the associate producer; costume ladies and prop men, electricians with bulging tool belts, scarcely dressed vapid-faced extras, account execs in costly suits, friends and relatives and toadies—but Fernando's uncouth smile is only for me, across the floor, leaning quietly against the opposite brick wall. Many producers may be milling about, but I'm the only one who produced anything for him.

His exquisite face!—that lovely, smutty, vulgar face, next to the white-script corporate logo: an obscene juicy-lipped sneer, a gleaming gap-toothed overbite bulging below an elegant, aquiline nose, those deranged, leering green eyes, the creamy skin ringed with thick and wavy black hair. He has the mane of a Tuscan gigolo, loosely slicked back with exorbitantly expensive French mousse.

Fernando has the face of a satiated savage, a wild beast who's just had his first blow job from a member of another species. Fefu the frenzied, Ferrus the untamed, Fernando the feral—he looks like a desert Tarzan, a child abandoned in the badlands by cruel, careless aristocrats and brought up by wolves, coyotes, kangaroo rats.

He is all of that, in a sense. Fernando, an only child, his parents dead, is surrounded by desert critters: his legions of fans; an army of promoters and profiteers from record labels, concert stadiums, advertising agencies and production houses; gorgeous girls primed to tender him their flesh, firm as green fruit, for an unspecified prize (few realizing how little value any one of their bodies carries, because such a dizzying plethora of them are on offer), and the fresh-faced rich boys anxious to be his best pal, his *cuate,* his *compadre,* hoping that some of Fernando's leftover booze, drugs, or women will spill in their direction (or at least a little of his luster, a palmful of stardust).

His pumped pecs quiver under the white silken shirt, cut loosely in the waist to hide the belly that has bulged of late. The black pants are still tailored tightly; some meat on his thighs and rear is in fact an improvement (at least in my estimation) over the notably scrawny body exposed in skimpy bathing trunks, on album covers and videos, throughout his teenage years. Fernando is all of twenty-five now, an alligator-skinned veteran. For more than half his life he has been as famous as the pope (pick a pope, any pope you can name). It's been a half-life of excess, abundance, lavishness; every whim, wish, and caprice has been answered at once. Fernando has completely forgotten what it's like to want anything.

No wonder he looks like the debauched son of Dracula. He's a roaring, shimmering, hopeless coke freak. His habit is so poorly concealed that as soon as he reached his twenty-first birthday, upon which day his album *Fefu: 21 Años* was released, wags were already calling it *Fefu: 21 Gramos*.

Which brings me to the reason that his glowering, snorting face, his sucked-off glare of grimy gratitude, his indecent smile, is being directed straight into my eyes. Fernando's face: the puss that thousands think of when in bed alone, as they rub their humid hands between their legs. Slender maidens in their first flush of nubility, and now older women as well, since he recorded the album of classic love ballads last year—*señoras* with dyed hair and thickened watery flesh, bitter matrons who haven't been touched in decades, fantasizing that Fernando is devouring them raw. And God knows how many desperate men and boys, panicked and shamed that they're thinking of Fernando and not one of his female counterparts—tattooed Ale Guzmán, Lucerdito, Trevi *la atrevida*, fill in the blank, Name That Pig.

Fernando is smiling at me because I left in his dressing room an onyx-and-silver box filled with four grams of the purest cocaine I could find. I did so at the instruction of my employer, Pepe Sosa, who owns Mexico's premiere production company of TV commercials and rock videos.

These shrewdly considered particulars, personal services, crucial *detalles,* are what separate Pepe from the rest of the pack. I wouldn't have bothered, or remembered, to procure the coke, even though last year, when we made Fernando's first commercial for Coke (the irony is so obvious I'm embarrassed to call attention to it), production was held up for hours—at $5,000 a minute—because the idol hadn't brought any drugs with him.

I was dispatched to find some, and frantically sped in my Jetta

all over Mexico City, from club to club. Finally I found some in
a ridiculous spot, since raided and closed, called El Modern (each
room had murals of fake reproductions of Picasso, Matisse, Klee).
Under a dizzying ersatz Mondrian, I made a connection, with a
scowling brown youth in a black leather jacket. (Was the scowl
personal? A couple of years earlier I had found him in another kind
of a bar and paid him to perform an act that most people would
find pleasurable. Still, that I could afford to pay him may have
provoked a kind of resentment.) When I came to him for cocaine,
the balance of power had shifted. Seeing my desperation, and possibly with a desire for revenge, he charged me an outrageous fortune for the drug. I paid instantly, gratefully. The dealer was
delighted, Pepe thankful, and, most importantly, Fernando functioned. The shoot was finished and I was a hero. I can deliver—
which is why Pepe pays me five hundred dollars a day, when I
deign to work for him. But I'm just a glorified messenger. Pepe
knows what needs to be fetched in the first place and is willing to
work 365 days a year, and therefore owns the company.

Fernando perversely grins at me, clutching the brick wall with
his long fat fingers, the white cursive Coca-Cola lettering at his
side. I mirror him with my own subdued version of smugness, the
soft smile of a kitten who quaffed a little cream. His pleasure is
mine. Am I flattering myself to think that he sees me as a comrade
in arms, a *carnal,* a secret sharer? I, too, am stunning—tall, slender,
black-haired, with intense aristocratic features. I'm only six years
older than he (although at thirty-one I sometimes feel ancient
enough to be Fernando's grandfather). I also have felt the voracious
desire of a multitude, and once dispassionately used this power to
partake of what appealed to me and discard the scraps. I, too, know
what it's like to be wealthy, privileged, at the top of a pyramid.

I envy Fernando. If he were to drop dead this instant, he would be deified—millions would remember him, forever. And me? I fear my memory would dissipate quickly. Sometimes I wonder if, had I any particular talent, I might have become a Fernando. No, people from our social class don't become entertainers—too vulgar, too public. It's much easier for me to entertain the idea of fucking Fernando, supping on his supple body, in its earlier bony stage or its present, plumper, weight-lifted incarnation. Could that ever have happened? Could it happen yet?

He begins to laugh. A spot of spittle forms at the corner of his mouth where the upper lip begins to curl. A studio full of executives and extras, technicians and technocrats patiently awaits his composure. He is being paid $2 million for his three-day participation in a sixty-second spot.

"Ferrus," says Pepe amiably from his director's chair. "When you hear the drums, just start to lip-synch the words, okay? You can do that, can't you?"

The smile disappears from Fernando's face. He—reluctantly?—looks away from me and over to Pepe. He's serious now, nodding. "Ready?" Pepe asks. Fernando nods his head vigorously, and assumes an eager pose.

The synthesized strains of "*Ven aquí*," his biggest hit, begin. But when the drums start to pound, his cue to lip-synch, he just stands there, smiling, and starts to laugh. This is the fifteenth take of the last shot in the shoot. It's past midnight. Perhaps I should have been more prudent about the amount of coke I left him.

At this point, I know I'll never fuck Fernando. With a pang, I realize it's too late. It might have been glorious, when he was a skinny, frightened fifteen-year-old, or even when he was twenty-one, still reeling from the potency of being able to get anything he wanted. By then he'd had so many girls that, according to those resolute rumors, he started to dabble in boys. We might have had one glorious night in his mansion in Las Lomas guarded by goons and rabid dogs. Or even become secret lovers in his white house with its translucent pool in a deserted nook high above Acapulco Bay.

But by now he is too far gone to feel anything. He has no desire, no eagerness, no passion. He's never been loved for who he is, only been fucked for being "Fefu." It would be meaningless to fuck him now, for what is sex without love? I had my share of it when I lived in New York. In those four years a staggering parade of bodies came to me—muscular and sweaty, thin and shivering, lank and angular, plump and succulent. I had to commingle with all of those carcasses to understand my own folly, my wretched vanity, and finally understand the power of love—love, which I am convinced comes no more than once in a lifetime. Particularly if the lifetime is abbreviated.

I can still feel the presence of those men around me, airily, like apparitions, which I suppose some of them are by now. As fleeting as those encounters were, I carry something of all of them inside me, although their legacy feels intangible, impalpable. So far.

"Ferrus, is everything okay?" asks Pepe. Round-faced, bald on top, a brown ponytail hanging limply behind, he wears a smile that seems carved in rock. But I know he's not in an amiable mood. This is the most expensive commercial ever shot in Latin America. Fernando says nothing, smiling sublimely, eyes closed, head nodding, his hand waving in front of his face, miming primed professionalism. "Okay," says Pepe. "When you hear the drums."

Once again, the synthesized notes of "*Ven aquí*" begin. The drums start to roll, and once again, Fernando misses his beat. Can it be that he's too far gone, *más allá,* to lip-synch the first five words of his most popular song, a record that sold into the stratosphere? He looks at me again, for a second, with absolute panic:

an open, frightened, defenseless face, a cry for help: a face I could love. Then he slips back into his safe, obscene smile.

No, I'll never be Fernando's lover. In his face I see the terrifying blackness of my own shortcomings, as I pathetically attempt at a young age to find resolution if not maturity. I feel it deeply, the regret I've just understood: it's not my place to love Fernando, but merely to be one of his myriad handmaidens.

"Can you hear the drums, Fernando?" I ask softly.

"When Victor found out I had AIDS, at first he was shocked, disgusted, terrified," says Verónica Vélez, her eyes ablaze. "He hated me. He hated all women. And he hated himself for having loved me. He got drunk, he got into a fight and nearly murdered an innocent man. Then his mother convinced him that I'm the only woman he's ever loved, and we had this beautiful reconciliation scene at my hospital bed. *Híjole,* but they made me up to look like a cadaver." Veronica's famous low, raspy cackle begins to emerge.

I can just imagine. Verónica Vélez, a soap-opera AIDS victim: in a frilly pink gown, her platinum blond hair pulled straight back, her face painted in slightly more pallid shades, perhaps a faint band of perspiration around her upper lip. A depiction of suffering on the level of a head cold. And redeemed by love, needless to say. She'd look like a pig, certainly, but a cadaver by no means.

She roars with laughter, burying her face in my shoulder. I wonder if her thick layer of peach foundation will rub off on my blue pima cotton. Verónica: known to her countrymen as *La Tetónica,* in deference to her unconscionably large silicone breasts, constantly exposed to the edge of her nipples, on album covers, soap operas, commercials. They are just the tip of the iceberg of her falsity: platinum blond hair from an expensive bottle, collagen lips, a set of absurdly straight capped teeth, whiter than pasteurized cream. Her reconstructed cheekbones and jawline. Her waist made tiny from rib removal and liposuction, above enormous haunches. Verónica looks like you could prick any part of her with a pin, and in an instant she'd burst, take flight, and plummet ignobly with an emphatic farting sound. But the falsest construction is the myth that she has a human heart, which pumps actual blood. There's nothing but Freon in there; Verónica pisses ice water.

We are sitting in a private salon overlooking the expansive garden of a restaurant I like to call La Hacienda de los Ostentosos. It's a brand-new palace on Reforma decked out to look like it's been fermenting in the same site since the seventeenth century— gloomy stone walls, oil lamps, waiters in long brown robes with the shaven bald spots of monks. The prices, for the most banal traditional Mexican plates (*chicharrón* in green sauce, cactus salad, stuffed chiles)—food you can get in any cafeteria for *centavos*—are astronomical. We have already been sitting here for two hours drinking cocktails.

There are ten of us—Pepe and Verónica, the director of photography, some Coca-Cola creatives and account execs, a bigwig from Transportación y Vialidad (to whom I paid fifty thousand dollars under the table to close traffic on a little stretch of the inter-city freeway for twenty minutes, so we could shoot Fernando careening in a jeep). Fernando was supposed to be here, but after we finally managed a successful take last night, he collapsed.

"But seriously, I think it's very responsible that we have an AIDS plot in a *telenovela*," says Verónica, assuming an expression of earnestness that makes her look more treacherous than ever. She usually plays villains on the soaps; *Pasión Salvaje* is a smash success because of the sheer novelty of her portrayal of *la buena*. "The peasants don't read newspapers, but they all watch us. So we're the only way they'll find out about AIDS." Most of us at the table nod in as unconvincing an impersonation of sincerity as Verónica's, as if we were all fascinated by the social ramifications of her soap opera.

One of the Coca-Cola people, in an almost incomprehensible accent, says, "And do they tell people to use condoms?"

He's handsome, in his mid-twenties, with a blond buzz cut and an oval face, round eyeglasses with transparent frames. He wears an unconstructed suit of pale cotton, under which he sports a black polo shirt. We stare at him uncomprehendingly, most of us because we don't understand, a few because we do.

"What did you say, my love?" Verónica asks him, offering this man alone the candid, suggestive smile that she usually reserves for twenty million people at a time. She bends at the waist, allowing him a better view of the cartoon roundness of her contrived bosom.

Now that he's attracted attention, he becomes charmingly self-conscious: he even blushes. "I just wondered if there was anything on the show about using condoms," he says in largely correct but thickly accented Spanish.

"Condoms cost the same here as they do in the States," Pepe says in a rapid-fire slur. "Most people can't afford them. And some drugstores won't even sell them, because condoms offend their Catholic morals."

Buzz-cut nods blankly. Did he even understand what Pepe said? Finally the waiter arrives with my third Mexican boilermaker: a shot of tequila and a beer. I swallow the hard stuff in a swig, chasing it with a chaste sip of Corona. I get up, mumbling excuses, and walk back to the restaurant's beautifully tended garden: fragrant grasses, daffodils, a few wide oaks. A peacock with a long leash attached to one foot pecks around, occasionally exposing his ma-

jestic plumage. I breathe deeply of the sweetness and light a cigarette.

Too early in life I have been forced to contemplate what is sig-
nificant and what is extraneous. I am plagued, literally, by every
minute I waste. I sit on a stone bench and look up at the hazy light
filtered through the leaves. I ponder another recent, regretful discovery: I will not leave anything meaningful behind when I die.
When I was nineteen, my parents, who always appreciated the
power of our northern neighbor, sent me to study at New York
University. There I found out what I was: a dilettante. My powers
of concentration are weak; my span of attention brief. I flitted from
literature to journalism to art history and finally film, barely grad-
uating.

I also found out what I was in dark discos and back-room bars,
and devised my personal soap operas, of no more consequence than
Verónica's. I attempted to sort out issues of love and sex and power,
breaking hearts, couples, and other earnest *ménages* in TriBeCa, the
East Village, Brooklyn, wherever the subway took me. I thought I
fell in love a hundred times before it really happened.

I left New York eight years ago, dazed, depressed, disoriented.
I learned that no matter how separate I may be from most of my
countrymen, I am above all a Mexican. I couldn't really connect
with my queer American brothers—most were far too swishy and
audacious for my tastes. Or else they were intellectual city boys
dressed as laborers: the sleeves of their lumberjack shirts rolled up,
marching in jackboots outside City Hall, earnestly ranting about
their rights. This made no sense to me: a Mexican is born knowing
that he has no rights. He either pays for his rights with hard cash,
or else he steals them, hoping to get away with what he has the
guts to take. And then he keeps his mouth shut about it. Discretion
is still the better part of valor here; a gay Mexican would never

dream of pestering a bunch of contemptuous politicians about his plight.

Further, I found that I am romantic and passionate—love is essential to me. I knew this even as I fell sway to the gay *yanqui* pattern, accumulating meaningless conquest after conquest, in true capitalist fashion. I came to realize that I made no sense in the States, that I'd always be a strange exotic, a hothouse flower, looking for a patch of humid shade.

Since returning home, I've found that the love I have sought is nearly impossible here: mostly it's fleeting and furtive, quietly desperate, found in certain bars and cantinas in the center of the city. The majority of my counterparts are grieving with guilt over their wives and children at home.

Beyond love, there is art. I would have liked to have painted or written, but I lacked the necessary discipline and deliberation. My only contribution to the culture will be pop videos and Coke commercials starring Fernando Fulgor. I have made peace with those sorrowful facts, but what racks me is the constant, morbid speculation about whether, even a year after my death, anyone will recall me. Besides my parents of course who will be tormented and probably go to early graves after the demise of their only child. But will anyone else give me a moment's serious thought, recollect anything more than an effete and dashing oddball, devilishly handsome in handmade attire?

"It's a beautiful garden," says the young man with the buzz cut and the casual suit, who has suddenly materialized beside me. He has a slender, wiry build, fidgeting hands and a comely smile.

I have a hard time with his enunciation, though, so I respond in English. "What part of the States are you from?" I ask.

He insists on answering in Spanish. "I'm from a place called Everett, in Massachusetts," he says. "Near Boston."

My heart begins to beat more quickly. The only man I ever loved was from Boston. "And Coca-Cola sent you all the way to Mexico?" I stammer.

"What?"

"You're not one of Coke's post-NAFTA emissaries?"

"I'm sorry, but I don't understand what you're saying."

Now I'm completely confused. "I'm not sure I get you, either. Do you mind terribly speaking English?"

He appears slightly hurt. "The thing is, I'm trying to learn to speak Spanish well," he says in his native tongue. The accent is delicious, honey to my ears.

"That's admirable," I say, "but I'm not going to be your teacher."

He laughs and sits beside me. "You win," he says. "You think I work for Coca-Cola, right?" he asks. "That's what you're saying?"

"You don't?"

"No," he says, shaking his oval face. "I'm actually in Mexico on a fellowship. I only ended up at this lunch because one of my professors has some obscure connection with Pepe Sosa." His voice is pure Jack Kennedy: I could lick and swallow the sounds. He gives me an off-guard smile, as if he read my mind. "Could I bum one of your cigarettes, please?" he asks.

I hand him the pack. "You can have anything you desire. What kind of a fellowship are you on?"

"It's a prize I found in a Cracker Jack box at Boston University," he says. "They're helping to subsidize my dissertation."

"Really?" I say, staring straight into his round glasses. "What's your dissertation about?"

"Have you heard of a poet named Thrush Hartley?" he asks.

I remember the name from my NYU days. Also something of

his story: a 1920s poet from someplace like Missouri or Montana who scoured the New York waterfront looking to suck sailor cock. Then he went to Mexico, and against all odds had his first affair with a woman, the ex-wife of an ex-friend. It didn't exactly set him on the straight and narrow: he hung himself in the bathroom of a cheap hotel in the Plaza San Marcos, at the age of twenty-nine.

"I know the name," I say, "and a few lurid details of the life. But I'm terrible about poetry. I'm far too superficial to have ever read it well. Or really at all." If I cannot dazzle with erudition, I can try to disarm with honesty.

"If it makes you feel any better," he says, "you're in good company. Only prose read poetry any more."

What? I only had three tequilas. "I beg your pardon? 'Prose?' You mean prose writers?"

He even laughs with a Boston accent. " 'Pros,' " he says. "Professionals. Mercenaries. The hired killers—critics, professors, grad students." We sit on the bench, smoking, facing each other, with mirroring smiles.

That voice, that sweet smile, those strange glasses! I have an urge to casually run my hand across his blond buzzed head. "So you expected to sit among a bunch of long-winded intellectuals, and end up staring into the twin tits of Verónica Vélez."

"That's Mexico," he says. "You never know what's beyond any door. André Breton called it the most surrealistic country on earth. And I'm not sure I'd rather sit with the eggheads. Verónica is . . ."

"You don't have to be diplomatic. She's a triumph of cosmetic surgery and public relations."

"Can you imagine what it would be like to fuck her?" he blurts out. "Like a tightly blown blow-up doll." He laughs.

"Excuse me?" I say.

"Excuse *me*," he says, and places a hand on my thigh, firmly if only momentarily. "I'm drunk. I'm not used to having three tequilas before lunch at—" He looks at his wrist, where there is no watch, and laughs again. "Jesus, it's probably practically dinnertime."

"You must be ravenous," I say.

"Do you think anyone would mind if I sprawled out under the table and took a nap till we eat?" He drapes his upper body across the bench, chuckling. "Would anyone even notice?"

I stand up in a flash. "You know what? You're too drunk to wait for lunch! Let's get out of here," I say. "We've done our bit! We've put in our appearances."

"I can't leave yet," he says without conviction.

"Yes, you can," I say, pulling him up by his wrists. "We're getting out of here. Not only are we going to get something to eat, we're going to do it in a locale extremely relevant to your research."

I drag him inside the salon. Verónica, unflappable and unbearable, continues to hold court. ". . . I seriously considered a marriage proposal from one of the former presidents. I won't mention his name." She clears her throat meaningfully. "My children would have had the best political connections. I also thought about marrying a genius, so my children would be geniuses. But Carlos Fuentes is already married!" Verónica swings an arm around her husband's neck, placing Pepe in a headlock and almost drowning him in her breasts. "And then Pepe came along. I decided to marry him so our children will have the best of both worlds—they'll be well connected, and geniuses too." She kisses his bald pate, leaving the imprint of her bright lipstick lips. How gruesomely sweet. Pepe looks like he wants to disappear.

"And don't forget beautiful," says one of the Coca-Coloids. Verónica blows him a kiss.

"Darling," I announce, brushing my fingers discreetly but rakishly on Veronica's neck. "This fellow is on a fellowship from Boston University, and has very limited time. I've promised to help him with research." I engagingly wave good-bye to everyone and wink at Verónica.

"But we've already ordered for you," she says.

"Then there will be all the more for you to devour, Verónica," I say.

"Pepe, I'll call you," says the student. I grab his elbow and drag him out.

We jump into my Jetta and hurtle down Reforma. "Someday you'll thank me for taking you away from all that," I say.

"Let me thank you now," he says. "I don't want to owe anything." He reclines in the seat, his sinewy limbs loose. "I feel like Alice in Wonderland here," he says. "I've only been in Mexico three days and it's been a perpetual surprise. Last night I was in a bar in the Plaza Garibaldi and three guys from the bus drivers' union picked me up and took me dancing."

"Indeed. And where did they take you?"

"Some joint called El Catorce. There were strippers of both sexes, and we paid girls in short dresses a dollar to dance with us. And some cops came in and all hell broke loose. We had to run out of there." He laughs.

"How romantic," I say.

"And then after, we were walking down Lázaro Cárdenas and a squad car came and picked up two of them. Just like that. Me and the other guy beat it around the corner. He insisted I take this medallion of the Virgin of Guadalupe as a gift." He pulls down his polo shirt and shows off a tiny tin emblem supported by a dirty string, on top of a lovely swirling map of blond chest hair.

"And how did it all end up?" I've had a few similar experiences that culminated drunk and horny in one of the bus drivers' beds, his mother snoring on the other side of a thin wall bearing a crucifix. Kinky, but I prefer a suffocating room in a cheap hotel.

"Just like that," says my friend, smiling. "He went his way and I went mine."

"That's all?" I ask pointedly.

"Yup," he says, smiling at me. "Ships passing in the night. Can I have another cigarette?" I hand him the pack. "I'm starving. I don't know whether to smoke it or eat it."

Swollen slabs of brown and fatty flesh—hooves and haunches, maws and jaws, cross-hatched tripes, deflated udders, unidentifiable viscera gleaming golden with grease. Stringy, squiggly, plump as pillows, flat as pennies. All on offer in a hole in the wall, protected behind a glass shield, kept warm under an infrared lamp. *Carnitas:* Mexican mystery meat. This is as deep into a pig as you can go, *puerco profundo.*

"*Échanos dos de buche, dos de nana y dos de nenepil,*" I charge the murderous Aztec in the paper hat behind the counter.

"*Con todo?*" he asks impassively.

"*Con todo,*" I say. He plucks out the most esoteric of the entrails and hacks at them with a hand cleaver.

My poet gapes at the ritual, his blue eyes panicky behind his transparent lenses. "You're kidding, right? We're not really going to eat this?"

"Of course we are. You're starving. And all the tequila you've drunk will kill the bacteria that terrify you."

"What is it?"

"Nourishment. Trust me."

The *taquero* hands us red plastic plates with three tacos each. The meat, stuffed within the floppy tortilla, is adorned with cilantro, onion, salt, and covered with a glimmering red chile sauce he doled out of a stone *molcajete* with a wooden spoon.

"Okay," says the poet. "Here goes nothing." He folds a taco into a tubular missile and greedily stuffs it in his mouth. "My God," he says, his jaws working, his cheek crammed. "This is delicious."

"Now look around you," I say. We're in a tiny tranquil plaza, amid flowering jacaranda and a dry stone fountain, a quiet oasis amid the hubbub of downtown Mexico City. We're surrounded by cantinas, seedy hotels, small shops. "Do you know where we are?" I ask.

He stares across the square. "No, but it's beautiful," he says. His eyes light up. "Wait a minute . . . the Plaza San Marcos! That's the Hotel Bajío!" The same lodgings where Thrush Hartley hung himself. "We've got to go in there!" he howls, the music I was hoping to hear.

An hour later, sitting on the floor, barefoot, shirtless, sweaty, the blond hair swirling across his greyhound's chest and arms of tightly corded muscles, he swigs from the bottle of Sauza Blanco. He slurs his words. "Ford Madox Ford accused him of 'fake erudition' . . . no way that a kid in his twenties with no experience could know anything about anything. It was just words arranged prettily on paper." He slurps from a fat, succulent lime, the juice dripping down his chin. He has removed his glasses and his blue eyes glower intensely. "He answered that there's a meaning beyond meaning, and that was what he was trying to find in his poetry. And that's my portrait of Thrush Hartley: these mobile circles of meaning, sometimes free-floating and sometimes concentric."

Circles of meaning indeed. If he lives long enough he will realize that there is no such thing as meaning, only fleeting sensations of love and pain and pleasure. To me, what's meaningful, even momentous, is that soon, I will have him in my arms. The wait—a minute or an hour or until the bottom of the bottle—is not the agony of wasted time but the pleasure of communion, the excitement of anticipation.

When we entered this dumpy room, reeking of disinfectant, with peeling paint, fraying furniture, water stains on the ceiling— the Thrush Hartley Suite—it was hot enough to bake bread. The poet didn't flinch as I stripped to my silk boxers, but kept talking about Mexico and poetry. The room is so torrid that it didn't take him long to remove his own shirt.

He makes me think of *the man I loved . . . those yesterdays . . . the one who got away.* How can I talk about Gregory without sounding like a maudlin song from a Golddiggers movie, the kind of music he listened to while painting? When I was charging around New York, I found him, boyish and muscular although ten years older than I. A painter with a delicious Boston accent, identical to the poet's.

Gregory adored me, cooked me hearty and fattening meals, dragged me tirelessly to galleries, obsessively sketched me in the nude. I had never felt so consumed by anyone, and it frightened me. So I refused to have sex with him. We lay in bed for entire afternoons, listening to Mozart, talking about Raphael and Leonardo and Titian (this was my art history phase). He thought that by withholding sex I was being cruel—and I suppose I was, recounting my idiotic adventures with platoons of other men—but I swear that I thought I was showing him the profundity of my love.

It is one of my great regrets that I never had sex with Gregory, despite the fact that he became one of the early casualties of the disease that had so recently been given a strange, initialed name.

I not only ignored but laughed about the clarion call of AIDS. Not because Gregory and I had never fucked, but because it struck me as an absurd American hoax, a joke, a scam. A reflection of the gringos' typical vacillation between guilt and licentiousness, prurience and puritanism. Let's have as much sex as we can, and then feel so ashamed that we die.

I couldn't see any point in getting worked up about a lousy little virus. People in my country are Catholic and fatalistic: we die of something every minute of every day—cancer, heart disease, or traffic accidents, but also microbes, bacteria, even dysentery. We count fatal amoebae among our most intimate friends.

Of course the great majority of Mexicans who shit themselves to extinction are poor—but the poorer you are, the more deeply you believe, concluding that you'll go on to a better place. The rest of us grab everything we can, while we can, and ultimately take our lumps. We live for today, laughing at death—at least until we're at its doorstep.

Before I left New York, surrounded by paranoia and fear, I became confused. I refused to take an HIV test, but I found a doctor, a little bald man with a bushy black beard and tiny rimless glasses, who was conducting experiments that involved measuring blood. He perplexed me even further, and laughed when I asked if he did it with a slide rule. "Your counts are low," he told me later. "Alarmingly so. But on the other hand, we in fact know next to nothing about these cells. We can't say with certainty what the counts of a normal person would be. You may be perfectly healthy." He tried to convince me to take the test. I cried, and he suddenly flung his arms around me and gave me a sloppy, heated kiss. I fled and returned home. Eight years later, I'm still asymptomatic. I don't know whether to be skeptical, surprised, or gratified. My only treatment is herbal, with a *brujo* on the outskirts of the city.

My poet suddenly walks around the room excitedly, the bottle, almost empty, still in his hand. "My grandfather was a Czech immigrant who sold string beans in the North End," he pronounces. "My father's a machinist. And I'm getting paid to retrace Thrush Hartley's steps in Mexico City!" He laughs and marches to the open window, shouting over the sounds of traffic: "*Viva México! Viva la muerte!*"

"Hush," I say. "Don't make a scandal. Come here and hand me that bottle before you drink it all."

He obeys and stands over me, smiling as I finish the tequila. I set the bottle on the floor and place my hands on his slender hips, lean forward to press my mouth on his belly, tasting his sweat and hair and flesh. I push him on the bed and we awkwardly tussle; he's laughing and repeating, "My God, my God," but not resisting. I grab his belt and unzip him; he turns to help me pull off his pants. The poet's ass: narrow, round, impeccably white, two scoops of vanilla ice with hairy blond sprinkles. I put my arms around him from behind, embracing him strongly.

"Listen," he slurs. "Until this week, I have spent my whole fucking life sleeping between book covers. Do you know what I'm saying? I . . . don't have much experience."

"Have you ever been with a man before?"

He pauses. "Yes and no. Just . . . a little fooling around."

This is too good to be true. I lay on top of him, trying to overpower him as gently as possible. "So Thrush Hartley came to Mexico to have his first woman, and you your first man."

"I guess," he says. He gives me that lovely, defenseless look, like Fernando at the shoot yesterday. "You know, I'm scared of all of this. Just don't expect too much."

I kiss him on the throat. "Don't worry," I say. "Trust me."

★   ★   ★

It is night, and still outside; a low-watt street lamp illuminates the room. The poet snores and I smoke, in a tangle of cheap sheets, blood, sweat, and semen. Is this what it would have been like to fuck Gregory? Perhaps. Gregory, older and more experienced, might have been the teacher, the driver, the dominant figure, but maybe not—I have always been a stubborn power player. In any case, it was delicious, fucking my poet as if it were my last fuck on earth, as if he were Gregory. If it wasn't love it was at least a stunning simulacrum.

I am happy. I softly squeeze one of those hairy rounds and think, *I love him.* If he lives long enough, he will understand this—perhaps not until after I am dead and he's inherited my pain and confusion and illness. My regrets will be bequeathed, and transformed into his regrets. At least one person will remember me.

Prenuptial Agreement

*f*rom the terrace of the hotel you could hear the waves and smell the ocean. But the beach was pitch black and the moonlight obscured by dense and humid clouds. Roger was beginning to feel a not unpleasant growl in his belly, which he rubbed, producing an even more enjoyable sensation. "You hungry, baby?" he asked Yvonne. The dinner menus had been sitting in front of them, largely ignored, for half an hour.

"A little," she said in a low whisper, gazing into his blue eyes, which looked steel-gray in the candlelight.

"Then let's eat," he said. She liked his determination; he wasn't a wishy-washy type who needed elaborate negotiations for every decision. "Come on over here, hoss!" Roger called to the roly-poly waiter, waving to him broadly with his entire arm. At the bellow of Roger's voice, the terrace's few patrons looked up to see who was making all the noise. Yvonne, erasing a slight sense of embarrassment, thought: Let them look.

The waiter did as he was told. "What's your name, son?" asked Roger. The waiter was clearly his own age if not older.

"He told you before," said Yvonne brightly. "His name's Pedro." The waiter smiled, with a barely discernible bow.

"Paid-ro," said Roger, the name escaping from his mouth with a raspy drawl. "Paid-ro," he said a second time, as if savoring and then chewing on the word. Roger drank the last of his second double tequila, letting his neck stretch backward to drain the last drop. "I have a question for you, son," he said brightly.

"Sí, señor," said Pedro with a slight smile.

"On the menu here it says that one of the specialties of the *casa* is *enchiladas suizas*."

"Sí, señor," said Pedro. "They are very popular, very *deliciosas*."

"Paidro, let me in on a little secret," said Roger. "My wife talks more Spanish than me, and she says that *enchiladas suizas* means that these critters come all the way over from Switzerland."

Yvonne had only known Roger a little over twenty-four hours, and felt a rush of blood from her cheeks to her chest when he referred to her as his wife. "I didn't say anything of the kind," she purred. "I said they're called Swiss *enchiladas,* but that doesn't mean that they come from Switzerland, silly. It means they're done up in a Swiss style." She looked at Pedro with shrewd eyes and a frank smile. "Don't pay him no nevermind."

"So what gives, hoss?" Roger asked Pedro. "You put Swiss cheese on them fellers or you fly 'em in from Zurich?"

They spoke so fast, and with such strange mush-mouthed accents, that Pedro understood only about half of what Roger and Yvonne said. But he got the general thrust. In truth, Pedro hadn't the slightest idea why, how, or from where *enchiladas suizas* got their name. However, in a decade of waiting tables, there had been plenty of idle time, during which he'd developed standard patter about the most popular menu items for inquisitive gringos.

"*Enchiladas suizas* are the chicken *enchiladas* with the green sauce and with the cream, *señor,*" he explained. "They are named the Swiss because the green is on the bottom and the cream is on the top; they appear as the mountains in Switzerland."

Pedro's casuistry merely made Roger hungrier. "Sounds good enough to eat," he said. "Bring 'em on, boy."

"And the *señora?*" asked Pedro.

"Pedro," asked Yvonne, "how about the *tamales Yucatán?*" She gave him a playful look. "They wouldn't be the hot kind of *tamales,* would they?"

"No, they are not hot. The *tamales Yucatán* are the *tamales* with the pork and the chicken in the sauce of the tomato wrapped with the leaf of the banana."

"Mmmmmm-mmmmmm," she cooed. "Would you recommend those, Pedro?"

"*Sí, señora,*" said Pedro. He returned her gaze, knowing exactly where to stop, in the colony of earnestness, staring across the border at the domain of intimacy. "They are one of the most delicious plates of the restaurant," he said, somehow making this sentence, which he said ten times a day, sound as if he'd just thought it up.

"Then that's what I'm gon' have." She smiled warmly. Just as Yvonne sensed that Roger was beginning to feel slightly jealous, Pedro equitably redistributed his attentions.

"And *el caballero* likes another tequila?" he asked.

"*Sí, señor!*" Roger practically shouted. "Another *doble,* on the *doble!* And another Dos Equis, too!"

"*Señora?*"

"I don't know, Pedro," she said girlishly. "I think I might have hit my limit. But what the heck, we're on vacation. Just bring me another can of Tecate, honey."

"*A sus órdenes,*" said Pedro, and disappeared.

★ ★ ★

By the time the food arrived Roger and Yvonne had finished still another round of drinks, and the *trío romántico* had returned. They were two short and stocky men flanking a third, taller and lither, each dressed in an orange rayon shirt with a palm tree print, stiff white slacks, and white shoes with crepe soles. Their hair side-parted and held in place with oil, all three played guitars, dexterously crowding notes into each bar. In high-pitched tenor voices, they performed complex harmonies, lulling incantations of divine love. *Without you, I cannot live anymore . . . Our love, a ray of light that ignited . . . It doesn't matter if they say you are lost, with my true love, you will be found again.*

With the exception of *amor* and *loco,* Roger didn't understand a word they were saying, but the absence of language made his experience no less profound. The noise the musicians made was like a dream of what it would sound like if he died and went to heaven. The tones were so exquisite that for a while, there was no plate of food in front of him, no tequila, no fat waiter, and no Yvonne; it was just Roger and the three angels and their celestial music. His eyes filled with tears.

From the moment she met him, Yvonne had felt in her gut that there was something special about Roger. But when she saw his eyes well up, she fell in love, and could just about feel her broad hips melt into the cushion seat of her wicker chair.

She liked that Roger was confident and gruffly jocular; that he had strong, firm hands and was not in the least bit self-conscious, acting like a boy when his enthusiasm was sparked. And of course he'd earned a lot of brownie points a couple of hours ago demonstrating his ingenuity and avidity on the queen-size bed in their hotel room. But when she saw the saltwater in his pale eyes, any lingering doubts that he might be nothing more than a spoiled, dime-a-dozen, overpaid good old boy were quashed. Not only was he all man, he was capable of true feeling. She could go the long haul with someone like him.

She sighed quietly. She wasn't naive; there was little doubt in her mind that the difference between their ages would prevent their union from proceeding past the impulsive fling they were currently cementing. Still, after the sweat and the sea breeze, the Tecate and the tequila, she couldn't help but allow herself to wonder if a man capable of crying in public at the sound of three pretty guitars would also be able to see past a chasm of seven years.

And wasn't Yvonne a young thirty-nine, with a heap of loose curls as blond as they'd been when she was a baby? She had an ample body that had so far, to her satisfaction, defied any disasters of gravity. Furthermore, she knew how to drape it, with a bold print or a provocative slit, a deep scoop or a bare shoulder, elements that would call attention to its luckiest localities, and away from what she considered its less fortunate whereabouts.

She took the bolder step of permitting herself the intuitive guess that Roger was an old thirty-two. She'd been surprised last night when he had told her his age. It wasn't just his receding sandy hair, the purple smudges under his eyes, the thick cowboy mustache or that voice—really a lower-pitched, more gravelly version of her own, which sounded like the morning after a quart of Old Crow. No, there was something lusciously profound and ancient in his soul.

The previous afternoon, Yvonne had been standing in a fluorescent-lit conference room in a Dallas office building, asking ten cow-eyed Texans, who had nowhere better to be, which of two planned commercials—one with rock music and graphics, the other depicting a well-known retired linebacker sitting cozily on a couch in a living room—was most likely to propel them to buy something from Sofa Shed, one of Texas's largest furniture retailers. Roger, Sofa Shed's advertising director, watched her work raptly from the other side of a two-way mirror, but his interest was not exclusively professional.

After they finished, he discreetly placed two fingertips under her elbow and asked if she'd consider it sexual harassment if he invited her for a drink at Antares that evening. She had spent too many recent nights at home alone watching *Roseanne* reruns; it didn't take her long to say yes.

As the sun set, fifty stories in the air atop the Reunion Tower, next to picture windows with a revolving view of downtown, he loosened his multicolored necktie and ordered a bottle of champagne. "We've got one ground rule," he said. "We can talk about anything but work." She liked that.

"How is it that you're called Eye-vonne?" he asked. "It's spelled like Yvonne, right?"

If she had a dollar for every time she'd explained this, she could have retired. "The week before I was born," she said, "my mama saw a movie with Yvonne De Carlo called *Scarlet Angel*." It was the story of a New Orleans saloon girl who worked her way up to high society, which Yvonne's mother, who served platters of meat loaf and fried chicken in a cafeteria in Luling, thought would be an appropriate trajectory for her daughter. "And when she saw the name Yvonne, in her mind there was only one way to pronounce it: Eye-vonne. And that's what she called me, and it stuck all my life."

Roger beamed. "In high school did they call you Eye-vonne the Terrible?" he asked.

She'd heard this one before as well, and had a prepared response. "They sure did," she said, the smoke of her Salem issuing through her nostrils, "and in my case it was true."

Roger got a big laugh out of that. "I'll bet you're as bad as you look," was all he could think to say.

By the bottom of the bottle of wine, he had gone off on a jag about how the long hours at work left precious few for what he termed "simple pleasures." Some of the things that constituted the latter for Roger appealed to Yvonne (winter nights by a fireplace with a bottle of eight-year-old bourbon, Saturday picnics in the park next to the Dallas Zoo), while others made her want to grab her purse and claim a previous engagement (camping at Grapevine Lake; the Rattlesnake Roundup in Sweetwater, a hundred miles west).

"Well, Roger," she said, "I can hardly think of anything more simply pleasurable than sitting here with you among the stars drinking this bottle of bubbly wine."

She noticed that Roger's eyes smiled first, becoming attractively crinkled at their edges. Then the wide lips under the mustache, then the killer dimples. "I tell you what, Yvonne," he said. "Things are just about to get twice as pleasurable. Or four times as simple." He called over the waitress and ordered another bottle.

Yvonne liked men who liked to drink. Her father had been a boozer. At least that's what Mama said; she'd never met the man. And some of Yvonne's friends wondered whether or not she had a wooden leg that accommodated the quantity of alcohol she was capable of consuming. She was much more alarmed when, not long after the second cork popped, Roger proposed that they leave the following morning on a ten o'clock flight for a three-day weekend on a six-mile island sitting placidly by its lonesome in the Yucatán Channel, spitting distance from Cancún. He began to drawl about palm trees and coconuts and margaritas and moonlight, and Yvonne thought: This boy's playing me for something.

He read her mind. "Take it easy, Yvonne," he said. "It's just a long weekend; I'm not asking for your hand in marriage. Yet."

Marriage was a sensitive subject. She'd been there twice before, first when she was twenty-one and stupid, to a tractor salesman who had the decency to remove her from the Hill Country, but gave her a case of the crabs on their honeymoon, and then swore up and down it had come from the towels at the Monteleone Hotel. (Anything could happen in the French Quarter, he explained.) She divorced him a year later when, as if for an anniversary gift, he gave her a dose of gonorrhea. She'd married again when she was thirty-one and stupid, that time to a computer technician who was sweetly attentive to her but had the annoying habit of putting on her clothes and sneaking off to cocktail lounges in motels on Highway 20 whenever she turned her back. That ride lasted three years.

Since then a platoon of men passed under the bridge, but they were shopping, not buying. And now that she'd finally arrived at a point where she didn't consider herself quite so terminally stupid any longer, Yvonne had reached an inconvenient age where the men who took an interest in her were either married, gay, elderly, or charter members of the Losers' Club. More frequently than she liked to acknowledge, she medicated herself with bourbon at night in front of the TV, to fend off despair from the idea that she would spend the remaining nights of her life in just such a manner.

Roger noticed her reticence, changed the subject, and left her at her door a little later that night with a modest good-night kiss. At eight o'clock the following morning, he called to tell her he was ready to go with a tube of sunscreen for two. "How many tickets should I buy?" he asked. She claimed illness in a message to her boss, and packed a weekend bag.

★   ★   ★

As soon as the bellboy had closed the door of their hotel room, a spacious, air-conditioned box with a white couch, a plump bed with a beige spread, and a blue view of the sky and the ocean, Roger began to plant moist kisses on her throat while his hands traveled a labyrinthine circuit from the slope of her shoulders to the jutting precipices of her hips. She accepted this as a positive display of robust manhood, and indulged him his explorations for a while, but then resisted. "Hey now, bucko," she purred. "The sun's only going to be hot for about three more hours. Why don't we go outside and take advantage of it?"

He seemed ever-so-slightly peeved. "It wasn't the sun I was thinking of taking advantage of," he said.

"We have all night for fooling around," she said. This promising remark, a short but pointed kiss, and a temperate squeeze of his behind returned the dimples to his cheeks.

Roger appeared dumbfounded when she insisted on changing into her bathing suit in the privacy of the locked bathroom, but he got the idea when she reappeared in a transparent wrap slit all the way up a shapely leg and tied around her winningly protruding tummy, and a dark bandeau top, under which her wide nipples stood out in bas-relief.

They spent the remainder of the afternoon as she had hoped for, in a long, luscious tease, wearing sunglasses and swimsuits, drinking margaritas next to a crystal blue pool. She lay facedown on a deck chair and asked him to spread sunscreen on her back, and enjoyed the warmth and smooth hardness of his hands which, with her eyes closed, felt large and wide enough to cover her entire body. He sat up on the edge of her plastic deck chair as she returned the favor, distributing the salve across his broad back. She looked approvingly upon the firmness of his arms, chest, and legs, and the sandy hair sprinkled throughout. Spontaneously she put her arms around him and squeezed his soft belly, and she liked that he didn't try to stiffen it for her.

They lay there for a while, staring at the sun and holding hands across their respective chairs. "Life just about seems worth living, doesn't it," he said, smiling at her.

"Is this another one of the 'simple pleasures'?" she asked.

He stared up at the sky under his state-trooper Ray-Bans. "It's simple enough for me," he drawled.

Watching the sunlight ripple in the water of the pool, she looked at Roger, his face cryptic under the dark glasses. "Tell me one of your trade secrets," she said. "How many market research girls have you brought on this little journey here before me?"

"I'm not an impulsive person, Yvonne," he said slowly. "My father died six months ago, and I got to thinking about if I was wasting time, about getting right to the nut. That's why I invited you without any fanfare."

"That's okay," Yvonne said. "I'm here, after all. And I'm sorry about your father."

"Let's watch the sun go down from the terrace," said Roger. They went to their room. Yvonne showered, and then dressed in a white off-the-shoulder blouse and a flowing, knee-length print skirt. She was applying her lipstick as Roger exited from the bathroom, his hair askew from quick drying with the white towel he wore around his waist. "Hey, baby," he said, put his arms around her shoulders, and began to mess up her lipstick.

All men are demolition men, she thought. His penis protruding from the folds of his towel was an indication that, like a kid stepping all over someone's sand castle, he was set to destroy all she'd constructed in the last half hour with soap and water, cloth, paint, and hairbrush. "I thought you wanted to watch the sunset," she said.

"Look out the window," he said, continuing to kiss her. There was little to argue about—a dense cloud cover had rolled in; there was no sunset to be seen. "Okay, bucko," she said, and returned his kiss.

"I like it when you call me bucko," he said. She opened her mouth, put her arms around him tightly, and pulled off his towel. He led her to the bed and laid her down; she kicked off her sandals. Her eyes closed as he undressed her, she sensed his lips traversing her body and felt like a twenty-one-year-old bride—or rather, as she wished she had felt when she had in fact been a twenty-one-year-old bride. When her leopard-print panties were all that she had left on her body, he gently began to pull at their elastic waist.

"No," she said playfully, crossing her arms in front of herself and grabbing the garment. "These pants are not coming off."

There was the tiniest twinge of alarm in his countenance; he'd taken what she said at face value. Then he smirked and began to pull more forcefully.

"No, Roger," she said, holding on to the fabric tightly. "These pants are staying on my person." His biceps bulged; she heard the cotton rip, then lifted her hips to help him pull them off. He was beaming, as if they'd been the Dallas phone directory and not a three-dollar strip of fabric.

She smiled coyly. "You big old brute," she said.

If their coming together had been extreme and intense, it now seemed to Yvonne that he was as far away as possible, even on another planet, as he stared with wet eyes at the three guitarists, his untouched enchiladas growing cold. She said his name out loud, and either he didn't hear or he ignored her. When the musicians came to the end of the tune, Roger began to applaud fervently, the only one of terrace's dozen or so patrons to do so. He had a way of banging his fingers into his palm that sounded like thunderclaps.

"*Muy* bone-ito," he exclaimed, rising from his seat, the bottle of beer in his hand, and walked toward the trio. He stopped when he stood before them. "Thank you! Thank you! Thank you! What's all y'all's names?" he asked. The musicians looked at Roger blankly, and then at one another. He garbled very slowly to the plumpest one on the left. "What's . . . your . . . name-o?"

A lightbulb went on. "José," said the guitarist.

The thinner one to his right said, "Juán José. *Su servidor.*"

The third said, "José Luis. *A sus órdenes, señor.*"

Roger looked at them with confusion. "Can you beat that?" he said to himself. He turned and looked back at Yvonne, who was tucking into her tamales as she watched. "What do you know, they're all called José!" he cried. He again faced the musicians.

As a general announcement to the patrons and staff of the restaurant, he whooped, "I like my beer Dos Equis, and I like my guitar players Tres Josés!" He then turned to speak directly to the musicians. "Since all y'all are Josés, I reckon' you're gon' be Hose-A, you're gon' be Hose-B, and you're gon' be Hose-C." Roger chortled, but it seemed that his wit had been too sophisticated for the performers, who looked at him enigmatically, perhaps mistrustfully. He became anxious that they might misinterpret his good will.

To show them how deeply their songs had impressed him, he reached into the deep pocket of his safari shorts and found a quantity of coins that inspired the image of a pirate's trunk of buried treasure. How had he managed to accumulate such a hoard of silver in just a few hours on the island? He fished it all out in a sloppy handful; some coins spilled, jingling on the floor.

Kneeling, he dropped a loose pile of change at the foot of each entertainer. "Thank you," he said. "Thank you . . . and thank you." He straightened up. "*Muchas gracias!*" he cried, bowing at the waist, making a flourish with his hand. He began the walk back to his table, stumbling over a chair on the way. "*Muchas gracias,*" said each of the musicians in a small voice. They rolled their eyes at one another as they squatted to retrieve the gringo's money.

Pedro was clearing Yvonne's plate as Roger returned to their table. "*Hola,* Paidro!" he said, and gave the waiter a familiar pat on his round belly. "Another *doble,* por favor!"

"*Sí, señor,*" said Pedro.

"Are they the best or what?" asked Roger admiringly as the musicians began their next melody.

"They are the best," said Yvonne. Warily, she added, "Your food's gone cold."

The mirth disappeared from his face, and he uttered one dragged-out syllable: "Shiiiiit."

Yvonne smiled weakly. "You don't have to—"

He interrupted her. "Guess what, honey," he said. "I'm too old for a baby-sitter." He glared at her briefly, and then looked at the musicians.

For the next half hour, they did not exchange a word. Yvonne coolly smoked menthol cigarettes and nursed her beer while Roger drank more tequila and listened to the music. He mostly sat still, but reaching for his drink abruptly, managed to knock over a shot glass full of *sangrita,* a spicy, tomato-juice chaser, resulting in an elongated blood-colored blotch across the white tablecloth. Pedro and another waiter were there in an instant, gracefully covering the blemish with fresh linen napkins.

As soon as they were gone, however, Roger crossed his legs

brusquely, sending his plate of cold enchiladas to the floor, result-ing in a crash of smashed crockery and a pile of green, white, and beige sludge. As the two waiters and a busboy scurried over and began their cleanup, Yvonne watched Roger with his chin on his chest, a stiff hand over his mouth, repressing his giggle, like a wise-ass kid who'd burped in church. She didn't want to but believed he'd spilled the plate intentionally.

"*Uno más, amigo,*" Roger said to Pedro, holding up the snifter in which the tequila had been served.

"*Sí, señor,*" said Pedro. Yvonne marveled at the way the waiter kept giving him more booze. It was as if Pedro were conducting a cruel scientific experiment, or simply taking a perverse pleasure in seeing how drunk Roger could get, how much of an ass he would make of himself. Wasn't it part of his job to tell a customer when he'd had enough? In any self-respecting bar in Dallas, Roger would have been cut off an hour ago.

She produced a theatrical yawn, stretching one arm while she covered her mouth with her other hand. "I'm about tuckered out," she said. "How about you, bucko?"

Now he merely seethed. Finally Roger asked, "Did you or did you not just hear me order another drink?"

"Sure I did," she said, gamely attempting cheer. "But maybe when you finish that one . . ."

"Hey, Yvonne," he said, with a little smile. "I got me an idea." After fishing in his pants pocket, he produced the key to their room, and tossed it on the table in front of her. "Good night," he said.

Lulled by the darkness, a gentle breeze, and all she had drunk that day, Yvonne had fallen asleep by the time the snapping-on of the overhead light signaled Roger's return to the room. Wearing only a loose, short nightgown, she quickly covered her breasts with the top sheet as she realized that Pedro (who had already averted his eyes politely) accompanied her companion. In fact, the plump waiter showed a surprising amount of upper body strength—he was all but carrying Roger, with a stiff arm around the Texan's waist, and Roger's arm draped across his shoulder. In his other hand, Roger loosely held the neck of a bottle of tequila.

As they entered the room, Roger was in midsentence. ". . . a wood tank 'bout yay high," he was saying as he stretched the arm holding the tequila bottle up toward the ceiling, "maybe fifteen foot across . . . full of hundreds of big ole squirming rattlesnakes about three foot deep." He plopped down on the white couch. "They take 'em out one by one with a stick that's got like a trap for their heads, and then, WHAM!" Roger slammed a palm onto the low coffee table, nearly falling down in the process. "They bang them with a mallet and chop them heads clean off with a butcher knife."

Pedro stood stiffly as Roger slumped across the couch and took a pull from the tequila bottle. "Then they pass 'em over to Skinning Committee, which is all high school girls from the Junior Miss Rattler Contest." He laughed. "They're pretty little things, got on white butcher's aprons and rubber gloves. And they cinch the skin down the body of that snake"—Roger made a gesture that vaguely resembled masturbating an elephant—"and throw the skins in one pile. They gon' make boots out of them critters. And the meat goes in another big-ass bloody pile. They gon' fry up all that shit. Say, hoss, you ever eat fried rattlesnake meat?"

Pedro smiled in silence, apparently unaware that he'd been asked a question. "SAY HOSS!" bellowed Roger.

"*Sí, señor?*"

Roger spoke deliberately, pronouncing each syllable individually. "I said, did you ever eat fried rattlesnake meat?"

Pedro smiled. "*No, señor,*" he said.

"Then it's simple," said Roger, stretching his legs across the couch. "You're coming to Sweetwater, second week in March. You stay with me in Dallas. A hundred miles. Put your pedal to the metal, you're there in an hour."

Pedro smiled. "If God wants, I visits Texas." There was an awkward pause. "I go back to work now."

"Wait a minute, wait a minute, wait a minute," said Roger, "not so fast, amigo." He pulled his wallet from his pants pocket and, still sprawled, began foraging around in it. A pile of business and credit cards spilled on and around his chest. Roger sat up as he played with a fat wad of local currency. "Come over here, hoss. You did me a favor. So we're amigos, understand? I don't forget a favor, amigo." He held out two bills at arm's length.

"*Sí, señor*," said Pedro, impassively folding the money into his pocket.

"Let's cut out all that *señor* shit, you know what I mean?" said Roger. "My name's Roger." He stuck out an arm, and Pedro shook his hand.

"Royer," said Pedro, bowing slightly and taking a step back.

"*Royer*," said Roger, mimicking Pedro's pronunciation. "What's your name again?"

"Pedro."

"Oh yeah yeah yeah, Paidro. That's Yvonne over there. Say hello to Paidro, Yvonne." She gave the waiter a little wave.

"*Señora*," said Pedro.

"*Señora*, shit! I said her name's Yvonne, and she ain't nobody's *señora* around here! You get my meaning, Paidro?" Despite his permanent smile, the look on the waiter's face suggested that glass was being shoved under his fingernails.

Roger stretched out on the couch again, grinning, his eyes on Yvonne. "What kind of a *señora* you reckon she'd make, Paidro? She ain't nothing but a big-old, big-ass, big-teat moo cow. Ain't

that right, Yvonne? You a big-old moo cow. Say moo for Paidro."
He laughed. "Paidro probably wants to see them udders of yours."
He whispered intimately. "You gon' make his day, baby? Like you
made mine before? I think the boy wants to milk you, Yvonne."
He belched out a guttural laugh.

The waiter stood in silence, waiting for some kind of signal that
would allow him to leave. Roger kicked off his sneakers and
stretched his arms over his head. "Shoot, hoss, what you doin'
round here anyway?" he asked Pedro. "You want to fuck her? Or
you want to fuck me? I know what you want . . . you want my
purple rattler crawling up your old brown hole. You a faggot,
right, Paidro? All y'all a bunch of greasy faggots, right?" He was
sinking into the sofa.

"Y'all don't care what you stick it to, man, woman, or pig. I
don't mind. I'm actually what you call a liberal." He covered his
face with his hands and began to rub. "You know what I mean,
Paidro? Just so long as you keep your greaser hands offn' me and
my ass. Shit, but I have got a motherloving headache. A motherloving vise. Is gripping my. In all my born days, as my white-
haired daddy used to say." He let out a long belch and, mercifully,
went silent.

For a moment, Pedro and Yvonne looked at each other with a
deeply compassionate expression. She nodded her head and waved
him away with her hand. He left silently, with a bow. Roger began
to snore, louder than the Chattanooga choo-choo, thought
Yvonne. She briefly considered packing her bag and leaving. But
it was two in the morning. Where would she go? This might have
been the most pathetic moment in which she found herself in
recent memory, but she figured if there had been any danger at
all, it had passed. She tiptoed to the table, took a long pull from
the bottle of tequila, and went back to bed.

★   ★   ★

She got the sense that she had only just drifted off when she awoke to the sound of whimpering. She looked at the couch to find Roger sitting and crying, his hands covering his face. He wore only a T-shirt, and with his legs crossed Indian style, Yvonne noted that his penis looked small, lavender, and vulnerable. She was overwhelmed by a wave of pity for the man, and for a second considered taking it in her mouth to comfort him. Instead, she went over and put her arm around him. "Hey, Roger, it's all right," she said.

"I'm sorry." He wept.

"Hey, don't worry, it's okay," she said.

"I didn't mean anything by it," he said. "Any of it."

"I know, Roger," she said. She tried to pry one of his hands from his face, but he turned his back and buried his face in one of the couch's pillows, sobbing all the more violently.

"It's okay," she said, stroking his back with one hand and patting a bone white haunch with the other. "It's okay, Roger."

She remembered the tears that had welled in his eyes on the restaurant's terrace. She knew he was a complicated and confused man. All he needed was some kind of a stabilizing influence, a woman to keep him in line. That was all. Life was so simple; why was it so hard for men to see what was good for them? "I know it was just the tequila talking. Right, Roger?"

"Yes."

"You weren't really angry at me, were you?"

"No."

"Then why did you talk to me like that?"

"I'm sorry, baby." The crying jag abruptly ended. He was rubbing his face.

"You don't hate me, do you, Roger?"

Now he looked at her. "Oh, no, baby."

"You love me, Roger. Just like I love you. Right?"

"Shit, yeah," he said quietly, and rested a hand on her inner thigh. "I love you, Yvonne."

"You bet your ass you love me, bucko," she said. She pulled at his torso and embraced him. She gave him a few tender kisses on his face, sat back, and stared at him. He smiled; he was coming back to himself. She reached for the bottle of tequila, drank from it, and passed it to him. "And if you ever talk to me like that again, I'll kill you," she said. He laughed.

As he sucked the booze down, she decided to go for broke. What did she have to lose? "So what the fuck, Roger," she said. "You love me and I love you. We love each other. Why don't we just get married?"

She saw the glint of shock in his blue eyes. For a minute he was speechless. Finally he said, "So what the fuck." He drank again, and passed back the bottle. She figured he might be thinking about the grandchildren his father never got the chance to see.

Roger had played in a weekly poker game for several years and, as such, could appreciate a good bluff. He wondered if he should fold his hand and get fitted for a tuxedo, or call it and find a new market research company to do his focus groups.

THE RECRUITING OFFICER

*W*hen Rick showed up for work there was a message to report to the assistant deputy chief of station immediately. What a pain in the ass. Who did a little Yalie shitheel like Boggs think he was, ordering around Rick? He had a splitting headache, a runny nose, a sore throat, and hadn't had his coffee yet. He'd go to the cafeteria first and let the little prick wait.

On the other hand, it was already eleven. He was supposed to have turned up at the office at eight-forty-five. Rick decided to take care of his business with Boggs first.

Big mistake. Within minutes of arriving at Boggs's office, Rick felt blindsided, smacked upside the head, the legs kicked out from under him. It surfaced that the assistant deputy COS, twenty-six, chinless and balding with a blond fringe, had made the appointment to give Rick's ass a formal chewing-out. The throbbing in Rick's head was so severe that he only heard scattered pieces of Boggs's lengthy speech.

". . . your customary crap . . . failing to fill out your contact sheets and expense reports . . . you would have been sent a memo.

. . . The Company doesn't come down on a guy for having a drink now and then or even more than that . . ."

Rick snorted emphatically to detain the snot dripping from his nose, and searched his pockets for a Kleenex. He didn't have any. He ran a hand under his long, hooked smeller to wipe off any liquidy mucus residue from his handlebar mustache. With his squared-off, bottle-thick, plastic-framed glasses, Rick looked a little like a Groucho Halloween mask.

". . . you went too far . . . that shouting match with the Cuban at the embassy party. That was disgraceful."

Rick sat rigidly on the other side of the wood-paneled desk, a conceited smile exposing small, even, rodentlike teeth. "What?" he said. "Wait a second. I had a little spat. Who the fuck cares?"

"You were at a diplomatic function representing the State Department! Arguing with a Cuban attaché!" Boggs's voice went higher as he became agitated. The squeak grated on Rick's nerves.

"So the fuck what? He's just some little embassy pussy, in the cultural section."

"That's not the point, Rick! It's an embarrassment to everyone at the embassy. Need I remind you of the sensitivity of your diplomatic cover?"

"Oh, for shit's sake, Boggsy. What fucking cover? Half the people in this embassy are CIA and everybody in Mexico knows it." Rick's throat ached. He burrowed into his shirt pocket for a cigarette, removing one from the hole atop the packet. The harsh smoke would soothe the pain, and in the bargain irritate Boggs, who had asthma.

Boggs looked at Rick's dossier, spread open on his desk. "Your debacle of a few weeks ago doesn't exactly inspire confidence in your powers of judgment," he said, tapping his forefinger on a sheet of paper.

He referred to an incident in which a traffic cop had pulled Rick over for careening down Palmas at 120 kilometers an hour at two in the morning. At the police station, Rick had been too plastered to answer any questions, so drunk that he didn't even recognize the embassy's on-duty officer who'd come to fetch him.

Rick began to blow smoke rings toward the ceiling. "Boggsy," he asked, "did it ever occur to you that there's a method to my madness?"

A slight smile formed on Boggs's lips. "Frankly, no, Rick. But by all means, let's hear it."

Rick leaned forward in his chair and began to speak in a clipped singsong, as if to an obstinately sluggish child. "Okay, my friend," he said. "I am the Soviet Counterintelligence chief of the Mexico City branch of the CIA. Do you think I got this far by being a fuckup? By being a falling-down drunk? I'm in *Operations*. The Company pays me a nice buck to find KGB here in Mexico, turn them over and get them to work for us. That is my fucking *job,* my delightful and gratifying life's work." His nose itched, and his glasses slipped down as he twitched it.

"Now how do I go about achieving this *task*? I drink heavily in public, and make strange remarks, and even once in a while get into an embarrassing *altercation,* so that gossip will drift back to the fucking Russians that there is a loose cannon in the American Embassy. They will come to me, thinking they can recruit me. But here's the *rub,* Boggsy: instead, I recruit them.

"It's a simple process. That is how a guy in Operations works. That's *recruitment*. Okay? How a guy as young as you gets to be assistant deputy chief of station without knowing that is one of life's great mysteries. Whose cousin are you, anyway? In any case, there's your lesson for the day, free of charge." He snorted wet

mucus up his nose again, and a puddle of it fell to his throat. He
swallowed, and took another drag of his cigarette.

Boggs laughed, but due to the smoke in the room it emerged
as a wheeze. "So you're claiming your drunkenness is just an act."

"Right, Sherlock."

Boggs looked for another sheet in Rick's dossier. "The four
bulls at lunch. The multiple cuba libres at night. The seventeen-
hour vodka sessions with Igor."

"It's part of my job! You know that! You drink with these bozos
so you can cozy up to them and recruit them."

The words had begun to sound hollow even to Rick. In truth
his record spoke for itself. He had been in Operations for fourteen
years, since 1969. After his first posting in Ankara, his station chief
had concluded that "he couldn't recruit his own mother." Then
he'd been sent to work in New York. Although he'd run a few
big fish there, he hadn't reeled any of them in. And here in Mexico
City, he hadn't pulled a single Soviet plum. Nothing. *Nada.* A
gold-plated goose egg.

Despite the fact that Mexico City in 1983 was crawling with
KGB. They worked in the Soviet Embassy, and in the embassies
of all their satellites. All those "foreign correspondents" so eager
to report Mexican news to Albanian and Bulgarian press agencies:
more KGB. Those jolly business travelers with their schemes to
import chile peppers and tequila to Ukraine. Even some of the
musicians with the long unpronounceable names in the symphony
orchestras.

They were busy little beavers, too: they solicited moles in the
American diplomatic corps. They met with their American agents
in Mexico, because it was safer than in U.S. territory. Mexico was
also a passageway for the guns and missiles going to the Sandinistas
in Nicaragua, the FMLN in Salvador, and God only knew who
else in which other banana republics.

And if they had come anywhere near Rick's fingers, they'd managed to waltz right through. Sweat began to appear in a patch atop Boggs's crown, the only spot where his hair still grew with any thickness. His breath came out in labored short spurts. "Thanks for the lesson," he said. "Maybe you should become a professor after you go home. You seem to be a lot better at theory than practice." He removed a gray metal canister from his jacket pocket, uncapped and shook it, and put it in his mouth, deeply inhaling two spritzes of its contents.

"Finished, Boggsy?"

"I won't even comment on your bold-faced denial of your drinking problem. Except to inform you that not only will it find its way into your evaluation, but that a cable has also been sent to headquarters recommending that you get counseling when you return to Virginia." Rick noted that, now that he could breathe freely again, the young bureaucrat seemed to have warmed to his task.

"Is that all?"

"There's one other thing. Your affair with our little Colombian access agent. You know that's against policy. Her apartment was used as a safe house by various agents. She was also passing on worthwhile intelligence. Your dalliance with her put the brakes on all of that."

Rick removed his glasses and rubbed his puffy eyes. "Boggsy, before you stick your foot in it any further. Anything you say about Rosario, you're talking about the woman who's going to be my wife."

"But I thought you were already married," Boggs stammered.

Rick looked out the window at the palm trees that lined the street in back of the embassy. "That's been finished for a long time."

"Well." Boggs rubbed his chinlessness with two fingers. "That's about it," he said. "So you know what you can expect from your evaluation. I'm sorry I had to be the one to tell you about it." He closed the dossier on his desk.

"Don't be sorry," said Rick, taking a last drag from his cigarette and blowing the smoke directly at Boggs's head before stubbing it out in a black plastic ashtray on his desk. "Thanks for warning me. I'll be shitting in my pants all the way back to Virginia." He stood and straightened his necktie. "Now if you don't mind, I've got a message for your boss. Your boss who didn't have the balls to have this little chat with me himself. Who's probably not here because he's passed out or on a three-day bender himself. Would you tell him something for me, Boggsy?"

"Sure, Rick. What do you want me to say?"

Rick glanced at the folder in front of Boggs, with his full name printed on a label across its cover: ALDRICH HAZEN AMES. He'd never felt quite comfortable with those three pompous barrels, preferring plain Rick. "Tell him I said fuck you. With a Russian hard-on." He stood there for a moment, staring at Boggs with his triumphant rat-toothed smile.

In the back of a yellow cab bolting down Reforma, Rick tried to settle his jangled nerves. Boggs was just a candyass pencil pusher. Their whole conference had been a joke. It was nearly impossible to get fired from the Company. Rick's own father, also CIA, had been a far worse drunk than he was; by the end of his career, he napped at his desk most afternoons. Yet he'd stayed on, forgotten but not gone, retiring with a full pension at age sixty.

The scathing evaluation would be skimmed over by brass at headquarters and then sent to the back of a bulging file cabinet, never to be examined again. Back in Virginia, Rick would probably drift in limbo awhile, in "strategy," on "committees," until one bigwig or another, likely someone with whom he'd been through junior officer training all those years ago, decided to give him a more critical and engaged post.

"*Quieres un cigarro?*" asked Rick, holding up his pack toward the taxi driver.

"*Gracias,*" he replied, raising his right hand in refusal.

"You don't smoke?" asked Rick, lighting up.

"A little," said the driver. "But it's not my religion."

The problem was that Rick wasn't well connected. So he was kept off the fast track. All that mattered in the CIA was who you knew. It was as simple as that.

Sure he'd made a few mistakes, even big ones. But who hadn't? While stationed in New York, he'd left a briefcase full of important files on the subway, putting the life of a Soviet agent in jeopardy. Some Polish woman had found the case and called the FBI. He'd eaten shit for weeks behind that incident, yet here in Mexico the same thing had happened—an agent had left important papers in a taxi cab. They disappeared for good, but this guy's father-in-law was a division chief, so they'd let it slide.

"They say the pollution in Mexico City is so bad that it's already like smoking two packs of cigarettes a day," Rick told the driver with an exhale, the tobacco salving his aching throat and lungs. "So I figure a few more won't hurt me."

"*Sí, señor,*" said the driver. "A few more, a few less, it doesn't matter."

So I'm not the world's greatest recruiter. Big deal. I've had my shining moments, too. Rick had caught a Mexican mole in the embassy, who hadn't even been polygraphed by the numbnuts who'd hired him. But did that make a difference? No. The bigwigs were so humiliated by the incident that they'd just swept it under the carpet. And Bill Casey, working with less than half a brain by

Rick's estimation, was so afraid of a Communist insurrection in Latin America that he allocated no money or manpower to Rick's Soviet section in Mexico. How did they expect him to make a difference?

What was the point of his job, anyway? Every rational intelligence report supported the contention that the Soviets actually provided no tangible threat to the United States. The arms race and the cold war were bullshit mechanisms to keep the military industrial complex in place, and a bunch of gray and paunchy bureaucrats in their jobs. He felt thoroughly alienated. Sitting alone in his apartment the previous night, toward the bottom of a fifth of vodka, he mused that maybe he'd quit the CIA and go to live with Rosario in Colombia.

"Let me out here," Rick said, "at the Monumento de la Revolución."

"*Servido, señor,*" said the driver after pulling to a stop aside the enormous structure, domed atop imposing pillars. Rick paid him, left the cab, and automatically looking behind his shoulder to see if he'd been followed, walked down two blocks of a crowded side street. He made a sharp turn at the next corner and slipped inside the dimly lit, leatherette-and-chromium bar of the Hotel Diplomático.

"You know who killed your country?" asked Igor, swirling the last of the chilled vodka in his tumbler and then swallowing it in one gulp. He licked his front teeth noisily, savoring the taste of the liquor. "It was one man only."

"Let me guess," said Rick, reclining in his chair, his feet propped on another. He inhaled a cigarette between his lips while another forgotten one smoldered in the ashtray. Hadn't Igor and he had this conversation months ago? He was sure of it, but he'd forgotten the punchline. "Johnson in Vietnam. No, Kennedy. Or the guys who had him killed. No, wait a minute." Rick began to laugh scornfully. "You're probably going to say Truman for dropping the bomb."

Igor clucked his tongue, removing the bottle of Stolichnaya from the ice bucket and checking the sparsity of its contents before pouring himself some more. "They are little potatoes. They are angels compared to worst villain in American history." He checked Rick's glass as well, and though it was more than half full, topped it off. "It was Doctor Spock."

"Doctor Spock?" asked Rick, ash falling onto his lap. "On *Star Trek*?"

"Imbecile!" said Igor. He laughed throatily, a rough-skinned, thick-fingered hand on his belly. "That's Mister Spock! Played by distinguished Russian actor, coincidentally. I'm talking about Doctor Spock, author of notorious baby book."

Rick, doubled over, caught up in Igor's laughter, smoke spurting from his nose, asked, "What the fuck does he have to do with anything?"

"Because he is telling a generation of citizens to spoil their children," said Igor, banging a fat fist on the table. A few plates clattered. They were empty, except for one, which had a few remaining sliced cucumbers, sprinkled with lime and powdered chile. The wet red pepper made them look like someone had bled on them from a nasty shaving cut.

"The most subversive, the most heretical message in history of publishing," declaimed Igor. "It causes more harm than any book, except for maybe Bible. For forty years, all Americans are reading Doctor Spock, and they are pampering their children. Who grow up to become selfish, indulgent, greedy brats, thinking of themselves only and not of community. The children of what your people call 'the decade of me.' "

Igor, his round ruddy face growing purple, seemed to be enjoying himself immensely as he improvised. "And this army of millions of spoiled brats, my friend, will cause destruction of capitalism. When it comes time to fight, they won't know how. Blacks won't do it for you, like in Vietnam. It's the beginning of the ending. You'll see, Ricky." Igor looked behind him, searching for the waiter. He wasn't there, so Igor shouted at the top of his lungs, "*MARIO! TENGO HAMBRE!*" There were only a few other patrons in the bar, Mexicans in suits and ties of synthetic fabric, who averted their eyes and ignored the Russian.

A fiftyish waiter in a black jacket, his receding hair parted in the middle and slicked in place, was at the table in a moment. "*Sí, patrón, qué desea usted?*"

"We're hungry," said Igor, holding two of the empty plates in his hand. "*No podemos tomar tanto sin comer.*" He spoke Spanish well, although with the same thick accent with which he spoke English, trilling all his *r*s, whether single or double-barreled.

"*Sí, patrón, al instante,*" said Mario, grabbing the empty plates and hopping to the kitchen, where the cook had prepared a special cache of Russian-style goodies for their favored client.

"I don't think so," said Rick, lighting a fresh cigarette with the butt of the previous one. Between his sore throat and the smoke he was beginning to sound like an old lawn mower. "You know you guys are a lot more vulnerable than we are. We got more missiles than you. More bombs. More nukes. More ships, more planes, more men, more everything. And you're broke. Your system's the one that's going down. I wouldn't be surprised if the whole goddamn house of cards fell in . . ." He waved his hand, the cigarette between his fingers. "I don't give you another ten years." A look of contempt crossed Igor's eyes, but Rick mistook it for injury. "And you know I say this as a friend."

"Yes, I know you are my friend," exclaimed Igor, grabbing

Rick by the scruff of his neck and rubbing his forehead together with his counterpart's. "You Americans are so sensitive!"

They sat in silence for a few moments. "You're going to miss Mexico, my friend?" asked Igor.

"You read my mind," said Rick. "I'm leaving in two weeks." Most of the hacks in the embassy complained about the pollution, the crowds, the bureaucracy, but Rick liked Mexico City. He liked the palm trees and the yellow cabs, the spicy food and the flowing booze, the servility of the men and the availability of the women—his first year here he'd had three affairs in quick succession, before he'd met Rosario. He'd also banked most of his $44,000 salary, living like a playboy off a lavish expense account, in the style of Simon Templar in *The Saint,* as he'd always dreamed a spy should live.

"I'll miss you, my friend," said Igor. Yet his look was steely, not tender.

Already forty when he'd arrived, Rick felt he'd finally come into his own in Mexico. On that first posting in Ankara he'd been scared and green, so eager to be a good Operations officer that he'd flopped completely. The tension was heightened by Nan, his wife, also a CIA officer at the time. To accompany him to Turkey, she'd had to accept a demotion, which she bitterly resented and for which she'd never forgiven him. The assignment in New York had been more entertaining, but not as much as it might have been, after Nan discovered women's lib and their marriage began to disintegrate.

In truth, they'd had little in common. Rosario, Rick's new love, was virtually Nan's opposite: passionate where Nan was detached, opinionated where she was indecisive, strong where she was fragile. Nan wasn't weak by any means, but her power had been sneaky, indirect, from a passive cover. They'd hardly talked. In contrast, Rosario, like many Latin American women, kept her feelings in the front window, never held anything back.

Mario arrived with more fortifications: pickled herring from a jar Igor had brought, sliced and fried chorizo, beets in vinegar, and a concoction of diced potatoes, peas, carrots, and corn, swimming in mayonnaise, called *ensalada rusa*. "*Provecho, señores,*" he said.

"*Momento, Mario!*" said Igor. He held up the plate of *ensalada rusa* and casually flicked his wrist, as if ready to fling it like a Frisbee. "Are you trying to insult me, Mario? I thought you were my friend."

"*Ay, perdón, señor,*" said Mario.

Igor shoved the plate in Mario's hands. "The next time you bring me this *mierda*, Mario, I swear I'm throwing it on the floor! And I'll make you go down on all fours and eat it like a dog!"

"*Lo siento muchísimo, patrón.*"

"Boil the potatoes, mash the anchovies into a paste, and mix them with the mayonnaise!"

"*Sí, señor,*" said Mario, scurrying toward the kitchen with the offending plate.

"You know why Mexicans are so fucked?" asked Igor. "Because of the shit they are eating." Rick began to laugh. "Tortillas! Chile peppers! How dare they call that slop 'Russian salad.' " His baggy eyes betrayed deep offense. "I'm thinking of making a formal complaint to Miguel de la Madrid!"

The idea of Igor griping to the Mexican president about the name of a food caused Rick to laugh so hard the vodka spilled from his mouth. Igor jabbed at the sliced beets with a fork and stuffed a couple in his mouth. The juice dribbled onto his chin, toward his black turtleneck sweater. He poured the last of the vodka into his glass. "*MARIO! OTRA BOTELLA!*" he screamed.

A second bottle. After five hours of drinking, Rick felt woozy.

He had thought he knew how to hold his liquor until he met Igor, who could put away enormous quantities for twenty-four hours at a clip, and still seem as fresh and energetic as when he'd started.

A thin pallid character wearing a brown toupee in the shape of a cabbage leaf had arrived an hour earlier, about nine-thirty, set up an electric organ, and begun to play the popular standards of the Latin-American repertoire: "*Frenesí*," "*Piel canela*," "*Solamente una vez*." He'd invested in an instrument with an automatic drum machine to attract a wider public, but it hadn't helped much. Aside from Rick and Igor, more than halfway through their second fifth of vodka, only a few more Mexicans in cheap suits had arrived. At the next table, four young women with teased hair and high heels, boxy but soft in their tight minidresses, sat chattering with one another, waiting for one of the men to offer to buy a drink. Igor was flirting with a chubby one, whose smile was enhanced by a gold front tooth.

"Have some vodka if you want a drink," he said, holding up the bottle.

She wrinkled her nose fetchingly. "*Es que me sabe feo sin Coca*," she said, but nonetheless walked over with an empty glass. "*No quieres que te acompañe?*" she asked.

"Yes, of course I want you to," said Igor, pouring her a drink. "But what will my wife say?"

The girl smiled devilishly. "*Ella no tiene que saber nada*."

"She has a nose like a vulture," said Igor. "She'll smell your perfume on me a block away." He squeezed her ample behind. "Sit down with your friends, *mi amor*. My colleague and I are discussing important things."

"*Eres malo*," she said with a smile, and returned to her table.

Rick sat smoking his forty-ninth cigarette of the day, watching with amusement as Igor trifled with the bar girl. He'd had his share of such juicy figs in the last couple of years, particularly when he first arrived. Thank God women's lib hadn't made any headway in Latin America, he thought.

Igor looked at Rick through slitted eyes. "It's going to be tough," he said.

"What?" asked Rick.

"What you are saying before. The divorce."

"Yeah, but it's for the best, in the end. Besides, I've got Rosario."

"You really love her."

"God, yes." Rick took another drink. "You know, she's the first woman I've ever met who's smarter than me. One night we talked for two hours about *The Waste Land*. The only time I ever talked with Nan about T. S. Eliot was after we saw *Cats*."

"But what about money?"

"Oh, yeah," said Rick. "It's going to be messy. The bitch is gonna skin me alive. I'll be walking around Washington wearing a barrel."

"And Rosario's going with you?"

Just the thought made Rick feel better. "She'll be joining me in a few months. After I get the divorce sorted out."

"She's one classy lady. She won't look good in a barrel."

"We'll work it out," said Rick. His voice lacked the edge of confidence.

"I hope," said Igor gravely.

"Hey, it's not that bad."

"Rick, look at her side. She's from nice Colombian family. She's accustomed to live in big style."

"She's not rich, she's middle-class."

Igor said, "You Americans and your stinking 'middle-class!'

You have noticed what Mexicans are meaning when they say 'middle-class'? They have three servants and travel abroad every year, but they can't afford a Mercedes. Same thing in Colombia. You know she is thinking she marries a rich gringo. Or 'middle-class' gringo."

"Rosario knows I haven't got a cent. I've been honest with her."

"All Latin Americans think all gringos are rich!" Igor laughed, banging a palm on the table. "And look at how you are living here! Eating in best restaurants. Flying to Acapulco for weekend. Taxis everywhere. And all on expense account, no?"

Rick smiled sheepishly. "Well . . . it's Company business."

"The Company pays your rent here, no? You aren't spending a cent of your salary. She is probably thinking it's the same thing when you are back in the States."

When Rick pictured what life would be like at Langley, he flashed on a few images: a potty little suburban apartment, small rooms with beige carpeting, a built-in kitchenette with a linoleum floor. He saw himself sitting at a Formica-topped table, writing one check for the rent, and another for Nan's place in New York—until he could come up with a fat divorce settlement, anyway. He saw a Dodge Dart with birdshit on the hood, which was probably all he could afford to drive. A crummy motel room at some beach on the Maryland coast, where they'd go for a weekend in the summer, if there was any money left over.

"Look, Ricky." Igor gulped more vodka. "You know I think of you as brother," he said matter-of-factly.

"Thanks, Igor. I feel the same way."

"What I'm saying is. If you want." He looked at Rick for a long moment and spoke very softly. "I could make you rich."

Rick felt his face flush.

"You have access to information, I could be guaranteeing you and Rosario would never have to worry about money again. And your children wouldn't either. Ever."

Years ago, Rick had been caught cheating on Nan in the most humiliating way for both of them: with his pants around his ankles in a supply closet porking another CIA officer, and not a very pretty one, either, at a company Christmas party. Nevertheless, some years later, in New York, when he began to suspect she was having an affair with another man (he never knew for sure), he felt a keen sense of sadness and disappointment, a bottomless hurt, an abysmal emptiness, that overwhelmed him.

And that was precisely what he felt right now, looking at the pleasant pudgy face of Igor, his counterpart in the KGB, trying to recruit him. Rick had thought they were above all that. They'd been having these drawn-out drinking sessions periodically throughout his tour in Mexico City. Of course it had been Rick's original intention to try to recruit Igor, but he gave up on the idea because he thought it would destroy their friendship. He was under the impression that there had been an unspoken understanding between them that neither would ever make the pitch. They had too much respect for each other.

"How much would I be worth?" asked Rick.

"Well, I can't give you exact figure," said Igor. "In the long term, millions."

Rick doubted that: the Russians were notorious cheapskates. He had imagined being a mole in the past; probably every spy did, at one time or another. He'd seen himself walking around obscure corners of nameless cities, making little chalk marks on sidewalks or mailboxes, leaving packages of documents in woodsy areas in public parks. Or exchanging them for shoe boxes full of cash, in nondescript, unfashionable restaurants. In a sense it would be more exciting and of course more lucrative than what he was doing now. He'd probably be good at it. He knew he had the balls, and he was sufficiently discreet. The latter was hardly important: the CIA was so clueless it would be easy to get away with. It would be almost worth it to show all those smartasses in the CIA how brain-dead they truly were.

"You know, Igor," he said, "I've made my share of mistakes in forty-two years. I married the wrong woman. I made some . . . miscalculations on the job. I have a hard time getting along with my bosses." His voice cracked so he paused to light another cig-arette. "You've heard me bitch and moan about the Company. I think we've been doing some fucked-up things, especially under Reagan. I'm pretty disgusted with some of my government's pol-icies right now." He leaned forward so his face was inches away from Igor's, and said in a whisper, "But I'd never sell it out. *Never.* Okay? Do I make myself clear? You can go back and tell the boys that pull your strings that *Aldrich Ames is not a traitor.*" There were tears in his eyes.

Rick stood, squinting from emotion and cigarette smoke, re-moved a few large bills from his wallet and threw them on the table. "Good-bye," he said and weaved out.

Igor watched him go. It was no skin off his ass either way, but he was confident the American would come around. It was just a matter of time. The Mexican girl at the next table was giving him the big eyes, the light from the candle atop her table shining on her gold tooth. "*Ven acá, chiquitita,*" he said.

SHUTTERED

*d*oña Albita locked the wide wooden door of her ground-floor apartment and slowly walked through the cool, shady corridor. At the end of the passageway she arrived at a courtyard, bathed in blazing sun, which revealed the paint flaking from the cracked and crumbling stone walls, and a patina of blues, grays, and reds that illustrated her building's three-hundred-year history.

After sluggishly crossing the patio, silent except for a scratchy radio playing in a second-floor apartment, Doña Albita paused at the staircase and looked up toward the crossing lines of drying laundry hanging from cords attached to the roof. Before climbing the steps, she paused and let escape a couple of deep wheezes.

She was seventy-one, and every year it became harder for her to lift her legs, heavy from lack of use, up those thick stone stairs. She was so tired so much of the time that it was harder to get anything done at all. The only assignment that Doña Albita made sure she fulfilled without fail was to collect the rents of the twenty-one apartments in the building that her husband had left her when he died.

Most of her tenants could be counted on to pay their rent on time, with the notable exception of Mister Huguez, who was now six months delinquent. She sighed, pulled down the hem of her navy cardigan, and resolved to appeal to him for the umpteenth time. Supporting her unwieldy, jiggling frame on the wrought-iron banister, she set both feet, encased in blue, low-heeled pumps, on each step before assaying the next. Finally, she reached the top of the stairs and daintily patted her thick gray hair, subdued in place with an ample measure of gel. She walked to Mister Huguez's door and knocked sharply five times.

There was no answer. Not at home, she said to herself, perhaps he's out making money. More than likely, she thought, he'd be sleeping off the previous night's drunk. Just to be sure, she rapped on his door again. She waited briefly, and then turned to take the long walk back to her apartment. His absence was a relief; she got no pleasure from such humiliating encounters.

"*Quién?*" came the plummy, rasping baritone from deep within the apartment.

Her heart began to pound faster. "It's me," she called, waddling back. "Albita."

"Aaah, the lovely Doña Albita," he said, opening the door. He wore a colorless, primeval terry cloth bathrobe that had been picked and shredded to a mangy condition. "What a pleasure to see you this morning. As always." He spoke a nearly perfect, florid Spanish, but with a heavy English accent, drawing out the vowels and hardly pronouncing his *r*s at all.

Huguez was in fact Hughes, from south London, but when he arrived in Mexico twenty-five years earlier, more than half a lifetime ago, he found that the Mexicans insisted on saying his name in the same way that Anglo names had been bastardized when the Celts and the Irish crossed the Iberian peninsula at various historical junctures—Obregon for O'Brien, MalDonald for MacDonald, Miqueli for McKelly.

Hughes was the only man who flirted with Albita any longer; as such, he never failed to make her feel considerably younger. "And a beautiful morning it is, Meester Huguez," she said. She clucked her tongue, observing his mode of apparel. "It's after eleven and you haven't even left the house to see just how beautiful it is."

"I was actually finishing some work, Doña Albita," said Hughes, letting out a deep tuberculoid cough. "In point of fact I have an appointment shortly with the photography editor of an important North American newspaper," he said. "Eleven o'clock, you say? Dear me, I completely lost track of time. I must prepare, if you'll permit me. Is there any way I can be of service to you?"

Albita appreciated that Hughes's impeccable British politeness was not all that different from the immaculate cordiality of the Mexicans. He'd also once mentioned to her that each of their countries shared intimate, antagonistic relationships with the United States. So she looked upon him as a kindred soul. "Ay, Meester Huguez," she said. "It gives me great grief to even bring up the topic. But I imagine you already know why I am here." She lowered her voluminous chins but raised her eyes and stared at his face fixedly. The keenness of Doña Albita's small, piercing orbs—"the stare"—was her greatest weapon in the quest of shaming deadbeats.

Hughes's face, all too steeled to be shamed, was bald to the crown, where it was capped with stray tufts of gray hair. The semicircle of his high, wide forehead swung down to the protuberant knobs of his cheekbones, and then tapered, concaving to the pointy bulb of his chin. He had a turned-up nose with wide,

oval black nostrils, and thin lips surrounding prominent teeth. His
skin was pale, almost gray, except for asymmetrical pink flushes
here and there. His eyes were more gray than blue and, however
sympathetic, were no match for "the stare."

"Ah, Doña Albita." He sighed, lowering his head. Around his
gray chest hairs, he clasped his robe, which had no belt and threatened to open. "You cannot possibly be as grieved as I. Just yesterday I arrived at the offices of *Ovaciones* to retrieve my check,
and they assured me they had posted it weeks ago. So they asked
if I could be patient a few more days before beginning the process
of preparing another."

He shrugged his shoulders, his eyes downcast, his thin, inverted-
V eyebrows raised, a half-smile on his lips. The implication was:
You know the way things are in Mexico. "But I assure you that, within
a short period of time, I will have all the money that I owe you
and a month—no, two months' rent in advance." He had dared
to look up at her again, countering "the stare" with a warm gaze
from his milky gray orbs.

And he felt his landlady's scrutiny like a slap in his gray face: her
crow-colored eyes with the weighty bags underneath, her pursed,
fleshy lips. "*Ay,* Meester Huguez, *mi amigo,*" sighed Albita grimly,
shaking her head. "I wish you the best of luck today. *Que vaya con
Dios.*"

"Thank you," said Hughes. He began to shake involuntarily.
Against his will, his robe began to open. "Now if you allow me
to prepare—"

"Yes, of course," said Albita, averting her eyes. "Good morning."

"*Adiós,*" said Hughes.

She retreated and his door slammed. What a pity, she thought.

His body stiffened and shivering, Hughes began to sweat profusely. Such encounters were particularly traumatic the very first moment after awakening. He pushed his back against the door for a minute. His shuddering subsided quickly, and he walked past the kitchen where he saw Raquel, pudgy and naked, preparing tea. Thank God, he thought, wondering if he were more grateful for the tea or curly-headed Raquel.

He made his way to the high-ceilinged living room. The wooden floor had been painted dark red a decade ago, and the white, cracked walls were bare except for a couple of his photographs in cheap plastic frames. The spacious room seemed absurdly vast given the utter absence of furnishings, aside from a Formica-topped table and two spindly wooden chairs by one of the French windows, now open.

Hughes sat, looking out at the plaza. The old and the reprobate sat on green-painted metal benches festooned with pearl-gray bird droppings. Across the street, young girls stared transfixed at the voluminous white dresses in the bridal shop windows. A warm breeze caressed Hughes's face. He closed his eyes and enjoyed this modest pleasure.

When he opened them Raquel was sitting beside him, wrapped in one of his wrinkled and unwashed shirts, the teapot and two cracked cups on the table. Hughes was briefly befuddled—had he dozed momentarily, or had she entered at the same instant he closed his eyes? And then he became further confused about when he'd met her—was it four days ago or four months? Her name *was* Raquel; of this he had no doubt. Well, no matter. He had an incredible thirst; the tea would be heavenly. "I thank you a thousand times," he said in his fluid Spanish while pouring.

"It's nothing, Nigel," she said in English.

He took a first grateful sip of the scalding liquid—even better than tequila, he thought—and then realized that he'd expected her

to respond in Spanish. "How is it that you know how to pronounce my name properly?" asked Hughes in her tongue. She had
crooked teeth, and a heavy jaw, but was otherwise lovely.

She looked at him strangely. "Because I am an educated woman,
idiot," she said, laughing, in English.

Most Mexicans said Nigel's first name as if it were two Spanish
words: *Ni gel. Ni* meant *neither,* and *gel,* pronounced with that
hawking, expectorant *g,* was the goo that people used to tame their
hair. Neither *gel* nor what? *"Ni gel ni heaven,"* said Hughes into
thin air. He'd said it to himself a thousand times, but never out
loud before. Raquel didn't laugh, but he didn't blame her: it didn't
make sense, being neither Spanish nor English.

He drained his cup and fished in his bathrobe pocket for a cigarette, from a crumpled packet of nonfiltered Delicados. Hughes
put one in his mouth and offered them to Raquel, who crinkled
her nose and clucked her tongue. His hand only shook slightly as
he lit it. With the first inhalation, the dark tobacco mixing with
the sulfur of the match, his heart began to race. He was finally
beginning to feel awake.

Hughes filled his cup with more tea. It was now even better for
having steeped longer. He gave Raquel a soft pinch on the chin.
"For a Mexican girl, you certainly make an exquisite cup of tea,"
he said.

Her adoring smile was abruptly combined with perplexity.
"You showed me how, the night we met," she said. "Don't you
remember? At three in the morning, when we came back from
Maryann's party."

How odd, Hughes thought, her insistence on speaking perfect
English. He drew a blank about the lesson, although he vaguely
remembered Maryann's party, and meeting Raquel: she'd been
wearing a long-sleeved purple blouse and black skirt, or some such

costume. Everything added up, except for the mysterious predawn tea party. "Of course, of course," he said. "Sorry."

"You were drunk," she said.

"Doubtlessly." He raised his eyebrows and offered Raquel the same compassionate glance and half smile that he'd tendered Doña Albita. The technique was far more effective on Raquel, who leaned over to embrace him around the neck.

That was delicious, that was life. He guided her off the chair and onto his lap, gently placing his hands under the rumpled shirt and around the soft skin of her waist. He lingered over her wide amber hips. The chair creaked as she stood up. "Not in front of the window, everyone will see," she said, moving back to her chair.

He loved the modesty of Mexican women, however false. Stroking her satiny cheek, he smiled at her. "I'm so lucky you're here, Raquel," he said.

Again her aspect changed—first a stab of pain, then a wry smile. What stunning portraits those two expressions would have made, with the hazy light filtering in from the window, if only he'd had his camera at the ready. "My name is Margarita, Nigel," she said.

Fuck all, he thought. How terribly thoroughly embarrassing. The pain on the right side of his skull, the one that came every morning without fail, began to pulsate. "Yes, of course," he stammered. "Naturally. How could you be anything but? Margarita: the fabulous flower and the classic cocktail. What did I say?"

"Shut up," she said, tucking him under the chin with, he thought, a bit more violence than necessary. His skull began to throb viciously. It was like being beaten with a red-hot hammer from inside his brain. "You called me Raquel." She sat in his lap again, grinding her warm pelvis into his, suddenly speaking in rapid Spanish. "Just who is this Raquel? How long have you known her? Is she prettier than me? Does she do this to you?" She moved her body and reached between his legs.

The pain was riotous, unbearable; Hughes could stand it no longer. He brusquely guided her off of his lap ("*Permiso,* darling Margarita," he said) and went to the kitchen for his customary treatment. The bottle of Ollitas and the *caballito* into which he poured the robust measure (luckily he was only shaking a little bit) were at the ready. He drained it at once, fiercely suckling; a few drops dribbled down his chin.

The first tequila of the day always gushed over him like a wave—briefly the violent torrential wave of a storm at sea (his body shaking tremendously), and then like a calm, cooling, and gentle wave, reassuringly lapping at his limbs like a reprieve from a woefully hot afternoon.

The pain in his head began to recede; soon Hughes would forget it had ever been there. He sniffed deeply of the tall, now empty shot glass. A powerful musk, dry and sweet at the same time. He ran cold water in the sink, rinsed his hands, and then splashed it across his face, blubbering mutedly like the spawn of a seal.

He remembered the appointment with Stewart Hinds and that photo editor from the *Los Angeles Times,* and looked at the clock on his stove. It marked the time at two minutes before twelve, the same as it had for the last five years. *Something* at least could be relied upon in this life. But what time *was* it? They were to meet at one at the Café Versalles. He padded to the bedroom in his ratty open robe, looking for his watch, or the clock, whichever was still functioning.

There he found Raquel, or rather Margarita, fastening a lace-trimmed black brassiere, already dressed in a crisp tan skirt and flat black shoes. Her sullen expression and the thought of her leaving made him hungry for her. "Oh, don't go, darling," he said. "Not yet, it's still early." He embraced her with some strength.

Could he get her to undress again and stay? And what if he could? He felt a fleeting but extreme jolt of anxiety. Then he reassured himself: women tended to be palliated by his abundant affection when his prowess faltered, rather frequently these days.

"For me, it's late, Nigel," she said. "I have to go to work." She pointed to the slender, black-banded watch on her wrist. "It's eleven forty-five."

At least someone knew what time it was around here. "But you will come back . . . tonight?" Hughes asked, cupping her face in his palms. He gave her a minuscule kiss and looked imploringly in her coffee-colored eyes.

"I can't tonight," she said. "My mother is becoming suspicious. She's wondering why I'm sleeping at Adriana's house all these nights."

Margarita was at least twenty-five, probably closer to thirty. Hughes marveled that so many Mexican women, no matter their ages, seemed hell-bent on convincing their mothers, if no one else, that they were virgins until they married. "Can't you think of something to tell her?" he asked.

Staring intently at the cracked mirror above the old oak bureau, Margarita pushed her white blouse into the waist of her skirt and then applied crimson lipstick. "If I think of something, I'll call you," she said.

"You can't," blurted Nigel. "My phone is *descompuesto*." It was actually not out of order but had been shut off two weeks earlier as a result of ignoring seven months of bills from Teléfonos de México.

"They haven't fixed it yet?" she asked. She scrawled a phone number in the mirror with her lipstick. "What will Raquel say when she sees this? Call me at the office before six. Maybe we can meet early. *Adiós, papito*," she said. She hugged him and touched her cheek to his, kissing the air so as not to muss her makeup. And then moved for the door.

"Wait, wait, darling," said Hughes, steeling himself for a dreadfully tedious transaction. "Can I please ask you one important favor? And I sincerely promise this will be the last time." After this initial chilly plunge, the exertion began to warm him as he entered a fluffy region of memorized lines: "As a consequence of the declining fortunes of the peso, some of the newspapers are, uh, I should say, have been, terribly late in their payments to me. So if it wouldn't be too much trouble, I'd be extremely grateful—"

"How much?" she asked. Her smile, her stridency, her cheer were gone. She looked at him with cold suspicion: he couldn't remember what she knew; how much he, or anyone else, had told her.

"A hundred," he said. "Fifty will do, really." The truth was that Hughes hadn't taken a single photo for six months. For a year before that, he had only taken pictures where he could use a tripod, because his hands had become so unreliable, subject to phenomenal spasms at any given moment. He'd survived thanks to the charity of friends, the occasional job from a sympathizer, the misplaced maternal instincts of susceptible women. Well. He'd be back on his feet soon enough. He'd had rough spots before.

She removed a crisp green-and-white bill from her purse. Two hundred pesos. God, she was generous. She could never, never know how grateful . . . what could he possibly say? "Thank you so much," he assayed, his eyes watering.

"*De nada,*" she said quickly, and left. Hughes preserved the image of her squeezable shape leaving, first solidly, and then ever more transparently, like multiple exposures.

He showered quickly, soaping his shriveling, wrinkling body, pallid with patches of pink, the two gray bushes at his chest and pubis, the flaccid genitals and the thighs, surprisingly muscular from so much walking.

Stepping out of the shower, he removed a bottle of tequila from the medicine chest, and had another shot, solely to keep his hands steady as he shaved. Looking in the mirror—the raised eyebrows, the sunken cheeks, the enormous teeth—he thought: not bad that a forty-nine-year-old man as ugly as you can still command a bit of the likes of Raquel.

He put on faded jeans, sneakers, and one of his least frayed shirts—clean if rumpled, blue with no collar, that he'd bought in flusher times at the crafts market in Morelia. He grabbed his portfolio. Should he wear his Nikon around his neck? Some of these newspaper chaps didn't believe you were a photographer unless you were tarted up like that feverish fellow in *The Killing Fields,* ready to do a somersault and land with the lens in your eye at the merest clatter of shellfire. No, he wouldn't bother; he couldn't stand the idea of appearing to try too hard.

Just as he was about to leave, he had an intense burning sensation in the bottom of his gut, imagining a long red worm blazing about in his large intestine. Parasites? Hadn't he been in Mexico long enough, and consumed enough tequila, to become immune to any stray amoebae? As the uproar intensified, he ran to the toilet, quickly pulled down his pants, sat down, and discharged his wet, acidic, blistering pain. It was sheer agony, as if all his internal organs were hemorrhaging at once.

Then torment spread upward from his bowels: a sudden flash of heat surged through his body. The recurrent ache in the right side of his head attacked again, gashing, bleeding, pulsating. It was especially hateful when it ambushed him like this, completely unawares. Sweat poured from his forehead. Hughes began to shake, and to keep from falling, sat on his hands, filthying them in the process. Then he doubled over. If he didn't drink, he would die. He got down on all fours and crawled to the sink, clawing at the tiles for the bottle of tequila atop the sink, his pants around his ankles, staining the floor and wall, spilling the liquor on himself as he drank. Then the pain subsided.

His breath and pulse returning to normal, he lay on the bathroom floor and looked at the tiles. *What a frightful fucking bore.* He'd have to wash and dress again before leaving.

After cleanup duty, it was a relief to be outside, along a crowded, narrow street of squat colonial buildings. Filing along the sidewalk, at five foot ten, Hughes was half a head taller than most of the Mexicans. "*Permiso, por favor,*" he said repeatedly, navigating around the white-painted newspaper stands and bright orange carts laden with sweets and cigarettes. As if it were the healing blue oxygen of the Magic Mountain, he greedily inhaled the fetid air, smelling of diesel and carbon dioxide, fried tortillas and sizzling lard, feces wet and dry. Confidence began to course through him.

He hailed and entered a *pesero,* an old minivan spewing black exhaust, bursting to the brim with stubby Mexicans ("*Permiso, permiso, gracias*"), where he stood crouched in the back hanging on a strap, gripping his portfolio with his other arm.

A half hour later the vehicle approached the cheerful, open-air restaurant. "*Esquina, bajan,*" he shouted at the driver, who abruptly braked and rudely jolted the passengers into one another. Hughes exited the stumpy vehicle and puffed his way across the street. Stewart and his colleague were already waiting.

"Sorry I'm late, the traffic," he said, catching his breath at the table, offering his hand first to plump, tired-eyed, brown-bearded Stewart, who remained seated, and then to his colleague, who stood to greet Nigel. He was tall and slender, with alabaster skin, wearing an expensive striped shirt open at the collar, freshly pressed blue linen pants, Serengeti sunglasses and enough gel in his black hair to grease a football field. He looked no more than twenty-five. Hughes pictured a six-foot slithering white snake, with a sprinting forked tongue. The two men had empty coffee cups in front of them. "Nigel Hughes," he said.

"Wayne Veale," said the young man energetically. Yet he'd given Hughes the limpest of handshakes.

"You're not too late," said Stewart, looking at his watch. "Only about a half hour."

Hughes laughed weakly. "In Mexico, that's shamelessly early," he said to Wayne, smiling and sitting. "It's quite frowned upon to arrive less than an hour after a scheduled appointment."

"*Comprendamundo,*" said Wayne. "So. Stewart says you're one of the best shooters in Mexico City."

He doesn't bother wasting time on small talk, thought Hughes. "Well," he said. "That's a great compliment, coming from Stewart. I, I think he's one of the best reporters—"

"Nigel's very modest," said Stewart. "Show him your book."

"I've been in Mexico over twenty years and have managed to get some interesting assignments." He passed the portfolio to Wayne, and found a boyish waiter beside him.

"*A sus órdenes, señor,*" he said.

Hughes looked with dismay at his companions' coffee cups. "*Tiene Ollitas?*" asked Hughes.

"*Sí, señor,*" said the young waiter.

"*Un doble, por favor,*" said Hughes.

"*Para los caballeros?*" asked the waiter.

"What did you just order?" Wayne asked him.

Hughes had hoped it would go unnoticed. "Tequila," he said.

Wayne looked at his watch and smiled. "Rock 'n' roll," he said. And to Stewart: "Ask him for another decaf."

Stewart said, "*Dos cafés más, un normal y un descafeinado.*"

"*En seguida,*" said the waiter and with a sparse bow was gone.

"Do you like tequila?" asked Hughes hopefully.

"I used to love it," said Wayne. "But I've been on the wagon a good year and a half."

Only an American, marveled Hughes, could achieve rehabilitated alcoholism by the time he reached twenty-five. By thirty, he would probably have gone down in the dumps again and made another spectacular comeback. While Hughes ruminated, Wayne went through the photographer's life's work with astonishing speed.

He was racing through the best years of Hughes's life: a portrait gallery of presidents, business leaders, and soap opera stars; a panorama of the temples and pyramids of Palenque; a study of Oaxacans with their grave offerings on the Day of the Dead. The facade of the pink sandstone cathedral at Zacatecas, shot at dusk—a picture used for ten years in that city's tourism brochures. La Princesa Rubia, the nineteen-year-old blond *rejoneadora,* at the very instant that, on horseback, she gored a fifteen-hundred-pound bull named Noriega. That one had made the cover of *Sports Illustrated,* and won Hughes a silver statuette from the Mexican government.

"Good shit," said Wayne. "What do you use, a Hasselblad?"

"Actually, I'm still, ah, amortizing my Nikon F." Hughes referred to a ten-year-old camera that he'd not yet repaired since it had broken two years earlier. His last pictures had all been taken with another camera, a Nikon twice as old but that had been built like a battleship.

"No shit," said Wayne, nodding. He licked his lips with a red tongue. "So you don't use medium format."

"Well, not really," said Hughes. "Not yet. That's my next investment, though. For the magazines." What bloody difference did it make to him?

"Too bad. We're trying to get all our photographers to convert."

"But, but, why?" stammered Hughes. His heart was starting to pound. "I mean, surely the quality of the reproduction in a newspaper can't, can't pick up the, you know, subtleties."

Wayne looked up, and although he hadn't removed his sunglasses, Hughes could feel the reproof in his eyes. "We've got state-of-the-art. We expect the same from our contributors," he said. He turned his attention back to Hughes's portfolio. He'd already reached the end of the book, where Hughes had inserted a few artistic images: the deserted dirt streets of the Indian village outside Querétaro, the scrawny child sitting by an even bonier dead dog; the gorgeous nude partly swathed in bandages, à la Manuel Álvarez Bravo. Wayne's eyebrows shot up at that one. Every man's did.

"Rock 'n' roll," he said. "That reminds me." He slapped Stewart's thigh. "What about those girlie bars? You down, Nigel?"

"Excuse me?"

Tired-eyed Stewart looked at Hughes. "El Jemma. El Closet. Bar Manolo," he said, naming nightclubs where fetching, scantily clad women, for a price, stripped naked, sat in men's laps, and squirmed.

Smirking, Wayne said, "Sounds like a real human interest story, you know what I mean? You down, homeboy?"

Hughes, breaking into a sweat, sat on his hands. They hadn't begun to shake, but he could feel it coming. "What you're proposing, well, I mean, it's an excellent idea, Wayne." He could feel the trembling under his thighs. "There's more and more of these places since the peso devaluations. Some of these girls are supporting entire families, while all their fathers and brothers are out of work." Thank God the waiter arrived. Hughes achingly watched his tequila atop the tray as the waiter first served coffee to the other men.

"Make sure this is the decaf," said Wayne.

Stewart asked the waiter, "*Éste es el descafeinado, verdad?*"

"*Sí, señor.*"

"*Éste, y no el otro.*" He smiled.

"*Sí, señor.*"

"*Gracias.* You're in the clear, Wayne."

Wayne said to Hughes, "I can't handle caffeine. I break out in hives, head to toe." Hughes nodded sympathetically, wanting to grab at the tequila from the tray. Finally the waiter set it down. Removing a hand from under his leg, Hughes said, "Cheers" and drank, with great self-control shaking little, managing to spill only a few drops. He felt better immediately. "Anyway." He sighed. "The thing is. It's a very easy way for me to get my camera confiscated and my nose broken. You understand?"

"What?" asked Wayne.

He felt his body now under control again. "Well, the customers are mostly bureaucrats and businessmen, and chaps who work for the government." He drank some more. "They don't tend to want to be photographed, you see. And the girls won't be eager to behold their faces in the *L.A. Times,* either. Some of them may have family in southern California, actually."

Wayne, removing his sunglasses, looked at Stewart. "What the fuck is he talking about?"

Stewart chuckled softly. "He doesn't want us to do a Pulitzer Prize exposé, Nigel," he said. "He just wants a blow job."

"For God and country," said Wayne, smirking. "Luckily there are some places where it's still politically correct."

"Oh, right," said Hughes, drinking. "By all means. They're quite amusing, really. Those bars, I mean, not the blow jobs. Actually the blow jobs as well of course." He laughed lightly, although he felt submerged, drowned, in darkness. He couldn't possibly have accepted such an assignment, but it was nice to believe he was at least being asked.

"So you're coming tonight," said Wayne.

"Thanks," said Hughes. "I'd love to but I've already got plans."

"Suit yourself," said the editor, and handed back the portfolio. "Good shit. Take my advice and get a Hasselblad. Your life will be simpler and you'll get more work."

"Right," said Hughes, finishing his tequila. It occurred to him that if he made the motions of male bonding and accompanied his companions to the bars-cum-bordellos tonight—courtesy of Wayne's *Los Angeles Times* expense account—he'd probably end up with an assignment, maybe several. And then perhaps he'd become a stringer, or even a trusted staffer, being sent all over Latin America to shoot rigged elections, coups d'état, crumbling monuments. At his advanced age.

Not bloody likely. He realized that it didn't matter whether he went with Wayne and Stewart, not even an iota. Not only was the meeting over, so was his career. Hughes understood with sudden clarity that he'd taken his last photograph. His decaying equipment was held together with Scotch tape and rubber bands. He still had his eye, but it was useless—he had no hands.

For what seemed like an eternity, he had lived off other people's good will, affection, generosity, or guilt. In a year he managed to run up a debt greater than he'd ever earned in any twelve-month period. Not only was he absolutely useless to anyone, he fought to survive off the blood of others, like a leech. The thought gave him the shudders, briefly sent him into a black bitterness. Thank

God the waiter was conveniently near. He'd take advantage of that expense account while he could.

"*Otro Ollitas por favor,*" he said. "*Un doble.*"

"*Sí, señor.*"

After the waiter brought him his drink, Hughes sat passively as Stewart and Wayne made their excuses, paid the check, and left. He watched them walk away, seeing their shadowy figures in several places at once, like a time exposure.

It was calming to be alone, watching the busy avenue, engulfed in the embrace of a gentle breeze perfumed with carbon monoxide. He savored his tequila slowly and smoked a couple of Delicados, eyeing the secretaries striding along purposefully, the young German tourists in harem pants and backpacks, the *bolero* on the corner eagerly buffing the black shoes of a gray-suited businessman.

This was the life! Why didn't he do it more often? When Hughes had first arrived in Mexico City, and for many subsequent years, he'd passed myriad hours in cafés and cantinas. You could be a *boulevardier,* a *bohemio,* for so little money. Then, a few years ago, in anticipation of the free trade agreement, the peso became artificially high, and prices shot up dramatically. As a matter of practicality, Hughes learned to do his drinking at home. The habit became so ingrained that he continued to do so even after the peso crashed and Mexico became cheap again.

For a moment he entertained the idea of drinking away the entire two hundred pesos Raquel had loaned him, but he decided to be frugal, ordering just one more double and swallowing it at a judiciously unhurried pace. He didn't know when, or if, she was coming back, or from whom his next advance was coming.

He thus peacefully passed half the afternoon. After finishing, he stood, clutching his portfolio to his side. He inched his way home on foot, through calle Independencia, a narrow shopping street, crammed with sidewalk vendors of leatherette watchbands, pirated videocassettes of American movies, used magazines piled high on the ground, stiff from rain and sun exposure. "*Permiso, permiso,*" he droned.

He began to sweat and feel dizzy, so he leaned against a wall. His stomach became full with bilious pain. Had that ugly parasite returned? His legs buckled; the ground seemed to be moving under him. Closing his eyes made him dizzy. It was the pollution, he thought, the ozone count must be particularly high today. He looked up at the gray sky. What time was it? He'd forgotten his watch. Where was he? Smack in between the Tío Pepe cantina and the Bar Florida. One bracing drink? No, he'd wait until he got home.

After another interval of dizziness—which unfortunately occurred as he was crossing calle Allende, nearly causing an accident—he made it to his building, his hands shaking slightly as he opened the front door. He walked down the dark corridor and bumped into the soft and jiggling figure of his landlady. Startled, English tripped from his tongue. "So terribly sorry," he said, and then quickly shifted to Spanish. "The charming Doña Albita. How are you?" he said.

"*Buenas tardes,* Meester Huguez," she answered stiffly.

"Listen," he stammered, "my meeting went very well today. I believe I can expect my *compañero* to provide me with a great deal of work . . ."

"Meester Huguez," said Albita. He felt her grasp his wrist in the dark, and lead him to the light of the patio. "I would like to have a brief talk with you." She had decided to read him the riot act, and fixed him with "the stare."

And suddenly found herself in a state of shock. Looking at his face—the high arching forehead, the prominent bones and sunken cheeks, the turned-up nose and round black nostrils, the naked teeth—she saw a merciless, skeletal death mask. "*Dios mío,*" she said, crossing herself and wobbling her bulk away from him, toward her apartment.

A sixth sense helped Hughes to intuit what had happened. He chased her awkwardly through the patio. "You don't understand, Doña Albita," he said, his throat faltering despite the determination of his words. "I assure you I'm not going to die here. As soon as I get back on my feet I'm going to look into the, the, teaching application." Albita had slammed her door and locked it behind her.

"I always wanted to finish my days as a photography professor," explained Hughes, breathing heavily, leaning against the cool wall of the dark hallway. "At the Chelsea College of Art. Or, you know, if not in London, there are some good schools in the provinces. Birmingham. Or is it Manchester? I don't know, even Scotland."

He realized he was speaking to no one. He had to get out of there. A walk, fresh air. By now the traffic, of cars and *peseros* and pedestrians, was almost impenetrable as people began to journey home from work. The stench of diesel saturated the air. Dark gray clouds filled the sky. The muscles in Hughes's arms and legs began to throb, and the right side of his head started to pound. He sweat and he shivered. Barely able to move, he grasped a lamppost, looking into the heavy sky, trying to fill his constricted lungs with filth. He felt he might have to vomit, or shit, or both.

A smooth-cheeked adolescent with narrow eyes jostled him, hard, on purpose Hughes suspected, and his portfolio fell to the ground. A woman nearly stepped on it before he accomplished its retrieval. "*Permiso, permiso,*" Hughes said, clumsily lumbering down the street. The first fat raindrops on his skull startled him; they felt as hard as hammer blows. He could barely walk; he had to get inside somewhere. Where was he? He only saw a blurry gray mass of buildings, stumpy figures and murky sky. With great effort, he focused his eyes: calle Bolívar, a few doors down from La Oreja del Toro. Thank goodness.

He stumbled into the cavernous room, decorated with murals of Spain and antique bullfighters' suits shimmering with silk and rhinestones. inside glass cases. The blood in his skull pulsated. He slowly moved between the tables. There was Charlie Townsend, a sleek, black-haired correspondent for the *Independent,* chatting up a slender brown berry in a coatdress. He saw Hughes but pretended he didn't, turning his head. The photographer felt stabbed with outrage but couldn't really blame Townsend—how many thousands of pesos did he owe him? Hughes saw a fat bearded figure waving to him from the opposite wall.

Hughes trudged to Stewart Hinds's table. "*Buenas tardes,*" he drawled, sinking into a chair.

"Hello, Nigel," said Hinds, licking *sangrita,* the chaser to his tequila, from his mustache.

"This is indeed a surprise. I thought you'd be escorting your chap to innumerable dingy fleshpots by now." His head hurt so badly that Hughes was surprised he could even choke out the words.

Stewart stared into his glass through now mirthful eyes. "Wayne's in bed in his suite at the Four Seasons, covered in boils. It seems he inadvertently ingested some caffeine."

"Oh, dear," said Hughes. "Bother." He noticed Townsend waving to him from the other table. Now that he'd joined Stewart, it was safe; he was not likely to ask him for another loan. Hughes waved back.

A waiter so stocky that he could barely close the buttons on his black vest arrived at their table. "*A sus órdenes,*" he said.

Hughes found that suddenly, miraculously, his various pains and his headache had disappeared. He felt cool and quite tired, but not unpleasantly. He let himself enjoy the sensation for a moment, staring at the back of the bar, toward the kitchen, at the white-clad counterman ladling *caldo* into terra-cotta bowls. His vision went in and out of focus.

"You want Ollitas or Hornitos?" Stewart asked.

"No, thank you," Hughes said. Odd: it was as if he were hearing another man's voice. "Just bring me a large mineral water. With ice and lime." Stewart looked at him suspiciously. "I'm parched," Hughes said, averting his glance.

"*En seguida,*" said the waiter, dashing off.

Stewart snapped his fingers. "Oh, listen," he said. "There's something I wanted to tell you." To Hughes it seemed Stewart was whispering; he could barely hear. He still had that easy, cool, and languid sensation. "You'll never believe it. The editor of the Sunday magazine called. She's finally interested in the cantina story. So we have to talk about which ones you're going to shoot."

Hughes and Stewart had been talking for years about collaborating on a photo essay about Mexico City's traditional cantinas. Their debates about which were the most exemplary, how many would make a representative sampling, and if there was ultimately a coffee-table book in the idea had gone on for so long that, for Hughes at least, the project had a mythic quality. He'd assumed it would remain perpetually unrealized.

The waiter came back with his soda water. Hughes squeezed a juicy lime in the glass and took a long drink. It made him even cooler and more refreshed. "Stewart," he said, "this may come as a surprise to you, or even as a disappointment." Strangely, he could barely focus his eyes on the other man. He was so tired he could hardly keep them open. "But after our endless circuitous chatter on the subject, in the end I don't think I'm going to be able to do the cantina story at all. I'd love to of course. And it would have been brilliant for me, up until . . . well . . . this minute, really." He saw that Stewart had a perplexed expression. Could he hear what Hughes was saying? "But it's just not a terribly good idea for me to be strolling from cantina to cantina, you see. I've decided to stop drinking."

There. He'd said the words out loud. It was exhilarating: as if he'd plunged into the North Sea on a bracing morning. Stewart looked positively horrified, as if he'd made a particularly gruesome confession. "Come on, old boy, it's not such bad news!" Hughes laughed. "No one's died." He lifted the glass to take another drink of the soda.

A crash, a thud: the next thing Hughes knew his throbbing ache had returned, this time in the back rather than the right side of his head. He saw the tubular fluorescent lights on the ceiling, and a circle of shocked faces staring down at him: Stewart, Townsend, the brown berry, the waiter, sundry strangers. I must have fallen, he thought. How dreadfully embarrassing. Where is my portfolio? I'll just have to get up. He tried, but found he couldn't move at all.

"Don't be alarmed," he said. "This happens from time to time. It's just a question of low blood sugar, you see. I need brandy, please, three brandies. Because of the sugar content." He was saying the words, but he knew that the faces didn't hear him. And, alarmingly, that his lips were not moving.

For some reason he remembered a time when, accompanying a reporter in the Sonoran desert, he'd got a stalled Volkswagen to run by wrapping dental floss around the carburetor linkage. And he flashed on miraculous Margarita on his lap in the drawing room. And the Princesa Rubia unmercifully goring Noriega. And then his name: *Ni gel ni heaven*. The white fluorescence of the lights overhead began to spread, until it encompassed the entire ceiling, the circle of faces, and finally everything in Hughes's field of vision.

Acapulco Gold

*S*ometimes Miguelito would sleep on the beach, where the constant din of the crashing waves lulled him into a heavy dreamless torpor. But he'd wake at dawn damp, shivering with cold, and a dry mouth full of filthy sand that he had no choice but to rinse out with saltwater.

Sometimes he'd find a quiet alley on the other side of the Costera, the wide boulevard that snaked along the perimeter of the shore, and sleep in a doorway's shadow, or in a patch of earth between houses in the hills above the city. There he might rest through the night, but would just as likely be woken by stinging insects or a panting stray dog. On a few occasions, one character or another, smelling of rum and sweat, was so addled with drink that he tried to grab the sleeping child and touch his body, imagining that Miguelito was a woman.

His favorite place to sleep was right on the Costera, behind a glass door in a boxy compartment that housed an automatic teller machine in a branch of the Banco Nacional de México. The crack under the door could make it drafty, and there were intermittent sounds of traffic on the thoroughfare all night long, but the size was cozy, and inspired Miguelito to pretend it was his own room.

He was especially comforted by the golden light that bathed the chamber, streaming from the huge illuminated arches of the McDonald's franchise across the street. Even with his eyes closed, Miguelito sensed the luxuriousness of that yellow bloom, brilliant as the morning sun that would eventually warm him.

Except when his stomach was jerking with hunger, Miguelito also enjoyed the smells of fat wafting from the restaurant, from the multitude of grilled burgers and deep-fried frozen potatoes that had been cooked and sold there on any given day. Once, Miguelito had asked a gringo for money on the street, and the man bought him a *"cajita feliz"* from McDonald's. Consisting of a cheeseburger, fries, and a Coke, it was the most delicious food he had ever eaten.

Various obstacles prevented Miguelito from sleeping in the cash-machine booth with any frequency. Much of the time the door was locked, and no one could get inside except for rich people who had special plastic cards they put in a slot to gain entry. Usually he was too frightened or ashamed, but once in a while, Miguelito would wait outside as the customers completed their transactions, and then dart in as they left. Their faces would turn into masks of nerves and confusion as they quickly tried to hide the money they had withdrawn, and his lithe, nine-year-old form snaked around them.

The lock on the door was frequently broken, but in those instances there was a uniformed guard on duty, who usually chased Miguelito away. If the boy was lucky, the guard would ignore him for a few hours.

Morning was his least favorite time of day. Almost invariably he woke at dawn, or even before, and that meant he would be hungry for three or four hours until he could begin to forage for something to eat—either from employees at cafeterias opening their doors, or women storekeepers who felt sorry for him, or from bags of garbage recently taken out to the street.

Miguelito heard knuckles rapping softly on the heavy plastic door of the cash-machine booth. "*Órale, niño.*" It was the voice of one of the more sympathetic security guards. "*Pa' pronto es tarde.*" He pulled himself up from the floor, and rubbed his eyes with a palm as he inched out the door around the skinny man in the loose blue uniform. "*Gracias,*" he said and moved on.

It was a little before six, still dark, with the morning glow beginning to appear over the hills on the other side of the bay. He stood on the Costera, blanketed in the yellow light of the Mc-Donald's arches. Each morning after sleeping in the cash-machine booth, Miguelito remembered the time he'd eaten there. He'd taken small bites and chewed slowly so the food would last longer. He vowed he would eat there again, as soon as he could save up ten pesos for another "*cajita feliz.*" It was useless to scavenge their massive garbage bins; they hired a private carting service to take away their rubbish several times a day, including the moment they closed at night.

Miguelito wandered along the beach, watching the waves lap the shore as the sun rose behind his back. The tourists in the high-rise hotels wouldn't wake up until a few hours later, except for a few *gringos locos* who got up early and swam, or ran along the sand, huffing heavily as the sweat poured down their backs. For a while, he sat under a thatched-roof *palapa* belonging to Memo's, a seafood restaurant where a waiter had once tossed in the air the carcass of a fried *huachinango* that had only been half-eaten by a customer. Three waiters in red shirts and white pants laughed as Miguelito jumped for it, but he'd caught it before it landed in the sand, and it had been delicious. He'd almost choked on a swallowed bone, though.

When he first came to Acapulco two years earlier, from a shan-

tytown settlement a few miles east, Miguelito, then seven years
old, had made friends with Julio César, a tough twelve-year-old
who hung around the *zócalo,* the central square in the old part of
town. On these hungry mornings, Miguelito tried to think of the
other boy's words of advice: *When you're hungry, the important thing
is not to think about food. Just wipe it out of your mind. Remember, the
mind is stronger than the body.*

Miguelito was certain that Julio César was absolutely right. But
unfortunately, he lamented, there was something wrong with him;
he was deficient in some way. Every time he tried to wipe hunger
out of his mind, all he saw in its eye was food, food, and more
food: round ceramic *ollas* full of steaming brown beans; baskets
brimming with hot tortillas; the burger from his MacDonald's "*cajita feliz,*" its thin layer of melted yellow cheese lying flat across
the meat, like a cheerful blanket atop a meticulously made bed.
He'd wanted to discuss his shortcoming with Julio César, the only
one of the gang of older *zócalo* boys who had made friends with
Miguelito. But Julio César had disappeared one day after men-
tioning some vague trip into the hills to make some money.

On the beach, behind the Radisson Hotel, there was a freshwater
shower where the guests rinsed the salt and sand from their bodies
before climbing a wooden staircase to the hotel's pool deck. Early
each morning, Miguelito would pass by the shower, and if no
guard was on duty, remove his T-shirt and, wearing only his jeans,
wash himself. Once in a great while, he would even use a bit of
soap stolen from a public washroom.

He'd learned to arrive before eight o'clock, when an athletic
young man who dispensed towels from a stand went on duty. He
wore white shorts, a white polo shirt, and a safari hat, and would
invariably chase Miguelito away, shouting and kicking at him with

his white sneakers. Miguelito hated him—he treated the boy as if he owned not only the hotel but the water in the shower and the entire sea.

The sun dried Miguelito quickly, and he put on his T-shirt. Some mornings it was so quiet that he was compelled to climb the wooden stairs and look at the Radisson's pool: crystalline, ovular, without a ripple. He would imagine himself diving in and expertly swimming laps, as if he knew how.

That morning he found he was not alone. An attractive woman sat in the shade reading a fat paperback book. She had ivory skin and long golden hair kept away from her face with a black bandeau. Smoking a cigarette, she wore dark round sunglasses and a black one-piece bathing suit. A white towel was draped around her waist.

At her side, atop a white-painted metal table, was a plate of breakfast she had hardly touched. Even from a distance, Miguelito could make out its contents: yellow scrambled eggs, refried beans, and toasted white bread slathered with butter. He had once seen a cartoon about a girl who could make objects move by mind control, and Miguelito tried to do the same with the beautiful woman's meal. In his mind's eye, he saw the eggs move in a mass through the warm morning air into his open mouth. Then the beans, and the toast. The food would stand there, suspended in front of his face as he ate it a mouthful at a time.

The woman held her cigarette between two slender fingers, the nails painted red, of the hand that held the book in her lap. With her other hand, she reached for a tall, nearly full glass of orange juice, brought it to her mouth, and sipped through a straw. Miguelito watched the contents sink slowly; he could almost taste its sweetness.

With a slow movement of her long white neck, the woman

looked up and noticed him standing across the deck. Her blond hair moved in the breeze. Miguelito's heart jumped. They looked at each other, transfixed, silent. Miguelito felt ashamed, imagining how the woman saw him: ugly, dirty, hungry.

But: maybe she would understand, and give him some of her food. She didn't seem to want it. Julio César, who scrounged from restaurants with outdoor tables, had advised Miguelito that *gringas* could survive on very little; they always left on their plates most of what they were served. Tentatively, he stepped toward her. She said nothing, so he walked slowly in her direction. He stopped when he was about six feet in front of her, looking at her cascading, wavy yellow hair, the slightly rough and freckling skin above her breasts, the enormous black lenses in front of her eyes.

"*Hola,*" she said in a low voice.

If he asked her for food, she would probably give him some. But what if she said no? He'd die of shame. He could reach for the plate suddenly, but then she might scream. Maybe he could walk to the table and tentatively stretch an arm toward the food; if she didn't want him to have any, she would have a chance to protect the dish. He was paralyzed by his options.

"What's your name?" she asked. Miguelito didn't understand, but he could tell she was on his side. Nor did he understand his desire: to sit in her lap, his head at her breast.

He heard heavy footsteps, and a deep voice. "*Qué haces aquí, niño?*" He didn't even look up to see the hotel guard; he just stole one more glance at the eggs and beans, and turned around and ran across the deck, down the stairs, along the sand.

Hotel guards were dangerous. When he first arrived in Acapulco, Miguelito had tried begging in front of the Hyatt. A man in a uniform, smiling in an avuncular fashion, promising him some coins, had taken him by the hand around to the side of the hotel, where he smacked Miguelito ferociously across both cheeks and, once he was on the ground, kicked him in the ribs.

Walking along the Costera, a safe distance from the Radisson, he remembered something else that Julio César had tried to teach him: *you don't get something for nothing.* You couldn't count on anyone to give you anything. When Julio César saw food on a plate, he didn't think, he acted. His risk became his reward, not anyone's charity. Miguelito reflected that if he had that moment to live again, he would have grabbed as much of the woman's breakfast as he could fit in his two hands and run.

Ten minutes by foot from the *zócalo* there was a concrete embankment that led to steep, jagged cliffs where, several times a day, from a ridge 130 feet above the sea, young men with sculpturally muscular bodies said a prayer and crossed themselves at a small shrine to the Virgin of Guadalupe. After, they would dive into the crashing waves below. Their plunges had to be precisely timed to the swell of the breakers or they would kill themselves along the craggy rocks.

As soon as the dives had been successfully completed, the divers' assistants, carrying empty Nescafé cans, would walk among the crowd of gaping tourists collecting coins and small bills in appreciation of the daredevilry. Meanwhile, the divers, their exquisite frames dripping with water, would climb the rocks to the concrete ledge and mingle with the crowd, shaking hands, chatting, posing for photographs.

Miguelito liked to go to the platform for the late morning spectacle and watch the crowds watch the divers. He'd once made the mistake of begging among them, but one of the assistants had grabbed him by the ear, taken him aside, and emptied his pockets, shaking him down for the three pesos he'd collected. He made Miguelito promise he would never beg there again.

Later, Julio César explained that they wouldn't gang up on him if he waited outside the periphery of the crowd, and asked them for money as they dispersed, after the offerings for the divers had been amassed. Sometimes Miguelito imagined himself in a few years, tall, bulky, and well fed, among the divers. First, he'd have to learn to swim, though.

Miguelito stared at the people gawking at the divers approaching their precipice. He could tell which ones were gringos—they were mostly tall and lanky, and even the fat ones were fat in a curvy way, rather than the squared-off shape of his countrymen. But there were always some Mexicans among the crowd. He spied a woman, stocky, with tight graying curls, who wore a short-sleeved blouse and a long, tan skirt. She carried a plaid plastic shopping basket loaded with food. Brimming from the top was a pile of yellow mangoes, but covered with wide black spots, which meant they were nearly spoiled and sold at a bargain.

He walked slowly toward the woman and, his heart pounding tightly, stood still behind her, so close that he could see the sweat and wrinkles on the back of her neck and smell the sweet soap with which she'd bathed that morning. The crowd was quiet, watching the four divers cross themselves at the altar and then stand at the ledge waiting for the exact moment to leap. Miguelito had selected the biggest of the exposed mangoes, the black spots on its saffron skin almost pulsating with sweetness. Deliberately, neither slowly nor quickly, he stretched his narrow arm and splayed his fingers atop the mango.

The woman sensed something behind her, a cat or a rat or a fly, and when she turned and saw the boy grab one of her mangoes and run, emitted a short scream of fear. *"Madre de Dios!"* she exclaimed. At that instant, one of the divers leaped. The crowd gasped en masse; no one even noticed her.

After Miguelito had swallowed every fiber of the fruit, sucked on the immense seed, licked the juice that had dripped on his hands and forearms, and only reluctantly thrown the corroding skin into the ocean, he walked slowly past the hulking freighters rusting with disuse on the boardwalk. He arrived at the *zócalo* a few minutes later, the mango a distant memory.

Because the plaza was preciously guarded territory, belonging to the tough boys who had lived on the streets of Acapulco longer than he, Miguelito approached with caution. But as it was only eleven in the morning, few people had gathered at the sidewalk cafés or on the wooden benches. A couple of old men in straw hats dozed, and an old woman had stationed herself outside the church to sell *milagros*.

There was one couple, though, sitting at a table in the shade outside a restaurant that had been named Meine Alten Freunde two decades earlier, in a swell of the owner's sentiment after a flood of German tourists had crowded his establishment one summer. These days few Germans came, and those who did tended to be unwashed, unshaven, and half naked, sporting backpacks and smoking hand-rolled cigarettes, ordering one, and only one, ten-peso bottle of beer. The proprietor nonetheless maintained the name, which confused tourists and locals alike, as the menu was strictly Mexican.

Miguelito recognized the couple as gringos. The man was big, his rangy frame settled uncomfortably in the white plastic chair. He wore a faded blue polo shirt, baggy jeans, and sneakers with no socks, and had a black fake-leather pouch around his waist. Miguelito thought the woman, with wavy blond hair and black sunglasses, looked remarkably like the one who had been eating her breakfast at the pool of the Radisson early that morning. In a loose beige romper, she sat writing on postcards with a felt-tip pen. Her fingernails were painted red.

A waitress came to their table and poured a cold Corona into a frosted mug for the man, and set before the woman a tall glass of orange juice with a straw peeking out of the top. The man searched for money in his pouch to pay the waitress. The woman continued to write, her eyes remaining on the cards as she reached for the glass of juice with her other hand.

The children who begged from tourists at the *zócalo* cafés were usually small, and usually girls, although the money they gathered was quickly expropriated by the older boys who handled them. The traffic of beggars was strictly policed by the boys, but when they weren't around, it was an unspoken rule that the location was fair game. Miguelito gave the plaza a once-over, establishing he was alone, and approached the couple.

First he stood next to them. Miguelito could see the man's eyes behind lightly tinted glasses; he looked over the boy's head toward the Costera and the sea. Miguelito couldn't tell if the woman, writing away behind her dark glasses, was looking at him or not. He was impressed by how much she resembled the woman of earlier in the day, but then so many *gringas* looked alike.

He held out a palm. "*Denme algo,*" he said.

The woman was astonished at encountering the same boy from the pool deck early that morning. The guard had told her that although the street boys in Acapulco might appear to be charming, needy urchins, they were actually cutthroat thieves, drug dealers, even murderers. She surmised the man was exaggerating, but now that the boy was by her side, she felt menaced. Had he followed her throughout the morning, all the way from the Radisson, without her noticing? Did he have a knife in his pocket? She kept writing.

Miguelito stood there patiently, resting his skinny arm atop the plastic table, his palm up and his fingers splayed. He looked into their faces, his eyes wide. Sometimes it was a war of attrition—the longer you stayed, the more frustrated they became, and finally they paid you to leave. "*Porfas'*," he said.

The man, made uncomfortable by Miguelito's presence but with grudging respect for his persistence, laughed. He drank from his beer. "If we ignore him, isn't he supposed to go away?" he asked.

The woman stopped writing and looked at the man grimly. In measured tones, she said, "He's working my last nerve."

They sat in silence a few moments longer, the man and woman staring at each other through their dark glasses and Miguelito with his palm spread on the table. "*Porfis,*" whined the boy. He looked from one to the other, and imagined what it would be like if they were his parents. All gringos were rich; maybe they'd eat at McDonald's every day.

"If you give them money, they just spend it on drugs," said the smiling man. "That's what they say. They're all glue sniffers."

"I'm sure I don't know what they do with it," the woman said.

Miguelito tried another tactic, which Julio César had pointed out to him as it was performed by one of the girl beggars. He looked at the woman's wavy golden hair, the color of sunrise, flowing below her shoulders. He raised his arm and softly stroked its loose ends. He had never felt blond hair before. It was the same as black hair, only stiffer.

The woman had a paralytic fear of being touched by strangers and began to hyperventilate. The man grabbed Miguelito's wrist roughly. "Just a goddamn minute, kid," he said smoothly, still smiling. "This time I'm gonna upper-hand you." He leaned his long, ovular face into the boy's diminutive one. "You can't be putting your mitts on people's hair you don't even know." Miguelito tried to free his arm from the man's grasp, but couldn't.

The woman, gasping for breath, said, "Give him something."

"Give him what?!"

"*Anything! Give him something and he'll go away, Frank,*" she said. It had been his idea to come to Acapulco. Who went to Acapulco anymore? She'd wanted to go to Bermuda.

Looking at the woman coldly, still gripping one of the child's wrists, the man opened his leatherette pouch, removed some coins, and placed them in Miguelito's hand, which was numb from lack of circulation. He released the boy, who ran to the other side of the *zócalo* before looking in his hand and counting the money. It was just enough for a Coke.

The *refresco* filled him briefly, but in the subsequent four hours Miguelito had no luck finding food. The shopkeepers on the unpaved streets behind the Fiesta Americana shooed him away, having handed out their stale rolls and spoiled fruit to other boys; the door to the kitchen of Memo's Restaurant was locked shut; and in the few garbage cans along the Costera, he found no food waste, except for orange and banana peels, which he wouldn't touch, and an empty bag of potato chips, in which he found a few crumbs. He stood on the street with his hand outstretched, but tourists and locals alike walked past him without so much as a glance, and then around him when he brazenly stood in their path.

Feeling dizzy, he sat down in the patch of dirt under a coconut palm, in a stretch of the Costera between a high-rise condominium and a recently constructed strip mall. He could smell grease in the distance: he wasn't far from McDonald's.

He thought of his father, whom he hadn't seen in two years, and began to whimper softly. He wanted to cry out, to scream with wretched pain, but his father had taught him that such behavior was unseemly in a boy. On the other hand, he had seen the man weep in agony after his mother went away. "I'm sorry," his cousins kept telling his father, clasping him on the shoulder. For Miguelito, they erased their grave expressions and put on cheerful faces. "She'll be back soon," they said. But the boy didn't believe them because he didn't trust them. His suspicions were confirmed: they were nice to him until his father left their shantytown shack to find work. Then they'd thrown the boy out to fend for himself.

He wiped his eyes on the short and fraying sleeve of his T-shirt. "*Tienes hambre, muchacho?*" A tall man spoke—a gringo, with close-cropped blond hair, aviator sunglasses, a tight black T-shirt, and loose white drawstring pants. Miguelito noticed that he had bulging muscles, like the divers, and that even the stubbly hairs on his chin were yellow. He felt embarrassed for having been caught crying, but at the same time heartened, for it appeared the man was offering help.

Miguelito looked at him hopefully. "*Sí*," he said.

All Miguelito's senses were engaged; so much competed for his attention. There was the brightness of the orange Formica, the chill of the air-conditioning, the glaring fluorescent lights. A north-of-the-border pop tune blared through speakers: "... *my baby's got a secret* ..." Through the picture windows Miguelito saw children playing, all extraordinarily clean and wearing new clothes, bouncing on the swings and slides and jungle gyms that the McDonald's strategists had devised to seduce them into begging their parents to bring them there.

A sumptuous meal sat in front of him, the nucleus of which was the largest sandwich he had ever eaten, two cheese-blanketed hamburger patties between a three-piece bun, with a collection of vegetables and sauces arranged among the layers.

Overloaded with such stimuli, Miguelito nonetheless considered that his new friend, the man sitting across from him in the Formica booth, the gringo with the golden stubble, who kept his dark glasses on indoors, was most deserving of his attention. Not only because the man was friendly, solicitous, and generous—he had bought Miguelito the meal—but he seemed to know the boy's father.

"He's not too tall, right? Not as tall as me. But a lot taller than you," said the man with a chuckle, exposing his straight and enormous white teeth.

"*Sí, señor*," said Miguelito.

"I told you to leave that *señor* stuff," said the man in his accented but fluent Spanish. "My name is Hunter, but my friends call me Rob." The boy had never seen teeth like Hunter's, which had been capped expensively by a dentist in Palm Springs. "And, uh, he's got a mustache, right? I want to make sure I'm thinking of the right guy."

"*Sí! Se llama Juan Hernández,*" Miguelito practically screamed. His father, like untold millions of Mexican men, had indeed worn a mustache. It had never grown in very thickly, but he felt that shaving would undermine his masculinity. Besides, razors cost money, which he never had.

"Juan, sure, he looks just like you, only older," said Rob Hunter. Miguelito lifted the tremendous sandwich to his mouth, which he had to stretch to its limits to take a bite. "Yeah, I saw him in Chilpancingo about a month ago." The name of the city had a familiar ring to the boy. He knew it was far, farther than the shantytown where he'd grown up, farther even than Pie de la Cuesta, but not as far as, say, Mexico City.

"What was he doing?"

"I saw him in a bar," said Hunter cautiously. "I bought him a beer in a bar."

"Did he find work yet?"

"Yeah, he got a job. A good one, too." Hunter paused, clearing his throat. "He got hired unloading trucks at a supermarket."

Miguelito struggled to see the picture in his mind: his father, at a loading dock, like they had behind the big Wal-Mart on the Costera, carrying crates off the back of a sixteen-wheeler. He slowly chewed on another bite of his sandwich. He was confused: did his father expect him to find his way to Chilpancingo? Or was he to wait for him here? "Did he say anything about me?"

"Sure he did," said Hunter, rubbing the boy's unkempt hair, and then brushing his knuckles against his soft cheek. "He said to be patient, and as soon as he gets the money together he's going to come and get you. It won't be long now." The boy's eyes brightened as he bit into his Big Mac, mayonnaise and ketchup smearing his cheeks.

"Mmmm," said the boy.

"It would make your *papi* glad to know you're eating well." Hunter leaned over with a napkin in his hand, wiped Miguelito's face with it, and smiled. "Keep it clean, little brother," he said. He grabbed one of an enormous pile of french fries, dipped it in the little mound of ketchup the boy had made by squeezing plastic packets, and popped it in his mouth. Miguelito smiled back at him.

"What do you want to do after you eat?" Hunter asked.

Miguelito thought of the lonely stroll along the sand and sidewalk that awaited him. "I'm probably going to play some video games," he said.

"Great," said the man, his capped teeth gleaming.

Hunter's excitement inspired Miguelito. "And then I might go swimming later on. In the pool at the Radisson Hotel."

"You like to swim?" the man asked.

"Yes, and especially I like to dive."

"I've got a pool in my house," said Hunter. "And I have a TV that you can play video games on. It's a thirty-six-inch color set, with *cablevisión*." Miguelito didn't know anything about inches or cables, but at his cousins' shack, there had been a black-and-white set that received grainy images from two channels. He had dreamed of colors. "Do you like TV?" the man asked him.

"I like the cartoons," said Miguelito.

"Come over to my house and watch. And swim in the pool."

"Does your pool have a diving board?"

"And how," said Hunter. "Finish your food and I'll take you there."

Before he got in the Jeep, Miguelito sensed that he was taking some kind of a risk by accompanying Hunter. But the sense of danger was overshadowed by the excitement of the ride. From the passenger seat, the wind in his hair, he watched the Costera soar past: the white hotels and condos erected to the clouds, the signs in livid color advertising fast-food outlets, the restaurants with their heaped platters and two-for-one happy hours, the minimalls and supermarts. And then, past the Hyatt, it all ended suddenly as the road snaked its way west, high into the hills. As they ascended, the boy had a flickering premonition that his life was about to change.

Miguelito had never been to this part of Acapulco before. The road led up to some of the most expensive real estate in Mexico, to houses with sensational views overlooking the entire bay. Here, an international network of movie producers and pop stars, politicians and drug dealers, money launderers and tax shelterers, stopped and smelled the roses, marveling at the spectacular sunsets, awestruck at what their money could buy.

With a key, Hunter opened the door of a heavy metal gate topped with jagged shards of broken glass. After parking the jeep inside the property, they crossed a short cobbled path to the dark mahogany door of the whitewashed stone house. He opened this, too, and cocked his head inside for Miguelito to enter. The boy's heart pounded.

The boy's consciousness was painted with the colors of shantytown shacks and the sidewalks of the Costera, and the little he could scavenge from them. He had never seen anything like Hunter's enormous light-flooded living room: white stuffed furniture, a low glass coffee table and an oak dining set, a high shelf with sleek black stereo equipment and an enormous television set. Part of Miguelito's foot, loose in his rubber flip-flop, touched the cool tile floor. It had only vaguely occurred to him that people lived in houses that didn't have dirt underfoot.

He was left speechless looking out the room's enormous plate-glass windows, leading to a patio with a transparent ice blue swimming pool, as big as the Radisson's. Beyond, the brilliant orb of the golden sun had begun its slow ascent.

"You *devil*." Miguelito quickly turned his head and saw another man, also blond, but pink and fat and jowly, wearing a purple polo shirt and an apron around his waist, standing at a bar next to the kitchen. The boy didn't understand a word of the man's breathily spoken English. "How *do* you ever find them, Robby?"

"Make up some Kool-Aid," said Hunter with a smile. "And find a pair of trunks for the kid." He switched to Spanish for Miguelito's benefit: "What do you want to do first, swim or watch TV?"

*   *   *

There had been no bathroom in the shack where Miguelito had passed his first seven years; he'd learned to wash himself in a murky lagoon. When he saw Hunter's bathroom he considered it nothing short of miraculous: he had no idea that showers, like the one between the beach and the Radisson's pool, existed indoors. He played with the two faucets, adjusting the temperature from scalding hot to freezing cold.

When he stepped out of the shower to dry himself with an immense yellow towel, he panicked as he saw that his jeans and T-shirt were missing from where he'd left them, on top of a straw hamper, and replaced by a pair of boy's black bathing trunks. Someone must have entered as he bathed. He dried himself and put on the swimsuit.

He walked down a hall toward the living room, past two open doors, which he looked in as he passed: immaculate white bedspreads and white curtains and white tiles on the floor. On cat's feet he crept toward the sliding window that led to the pool. Hunter's friend was in the kitchen, stirring a pitcher of green liquid. Staring at Miguelito through heavy-lidded eyes half-smiling, he purred something the boy didn't understand. Outside Hunter waded in the pool.

"*Ven acá*," he said. "The water's beautiful."

Miguelito stepped to the edge. He was bereft: he didn't want to disappoint his friend by telling him he didn't know how to swim. He felt a rush of tears, then anger with himself for his weakness. Millions of fish swam without anyone showing them how. He jumped into the water.

And as soon as he began to thrash his narrow limbs and swallow water, Miguelito found himself in Hunter's strong and capable arms. "It's okay, it's okay," said the man in English, smiling through his exceptional teeth. Miguelito got his first look at the man's eyes, which were as transparently blue as the water in which they waded. The realization that someone had been there to protect him, that he fell without touching bottom, the mighty sensation of having been saved, was wholly new to Miguelito. Feelings swelled within him, and this time he could not resist tears.

The noise of his cries was music to Hunter's ears. "It's okay," he repeated. And in Spanish: "I'm here. You're okay. Everything's going to be all right." The boy wept in his arms. He stroked Miguelito's wet hair.

"The first thing you need to know," the man said, his wide, strong hands gently holding the boy at his waist and lower back, "is . . ." But he couldn't think of the Spanish word for "treading water."

"I'm in the movie business," said Hunter. "Do you like the movies?"

Miguelito had only been once; he and Julio César had snuck in through an exit of the Cine Gloria. He remembered high-velocity car chases, tremendous explosions, even the demolition of a high-rise tower, not unlike one of the Costera hotels. The abundance of action in the film had made it a mesmerizing experience for the boy despite the fact that he could neither understand the dialogue nor read the subtitles.

Had he actually said any of this to Hunter, or only thought it? Miguelito felt his mind playing tricks on him, and odd sensations in his body. He was fiercely hot underneath the white terry cloth robe Hunter and his friend, *el gordo,* had loaned him. And he could actually feel the blood vibrating, palpitating, swimming in his veins and underneath his skin. From the drawing in the *lotería* card, he knew what his heart looked like: a red fist clenched tightly, with blue veins popping up on top. He could feel his own beating inside his chest. Seeing the image, he laughed.

"All boys love the movies, silly," said Hunter's fat friend in a singsong, eyeing Miguelito with affection. He was funny, thought the boy. It was too bad he couldn't speak Spanish.

"I went once," said Miguelito in a small voice. The two men, sitting together on the enormous couch, stared at him, akimbo on the recliner, awaiting the rest of his sentence. They looked so funny—the two smiling golden-haired gringos looking at him attentively—that he almost laughed, abruptly forgetting the explosion he was going to describe. He felt embarrassed, so he smiled and drank some more of the green drink. It was syrupy sweet with an imploding tartness underneath—his third glass. This was Miguelito's first experience of excess; he'd never had three glasses of anything before. The men drank a grown-up drink, amber liquid from glasses with ice.

"Would you like to see one of the movies I made?" asked Hunter.

Miguelito remembered the blast that felled the building. With great enthusiasm, he made a rumbling sound and spread his arms. Hunter and his friend could see his little ribs poking under his chest where the robe opened. "He's *so* precious," said *el gordo*. The boy erupted in laughter and drank some more.

Hunter popped the cassette into the machine, sat on the couch, and said, "Come here. We'll all watch together." The boy eagerly ran to the sofa, and jumped in between the two men with a voluntary bounce. He realized that he had forgotten his green drink on the table by the recliner, and decided to go get it, but had the most peculiar sensation: he saw his own skinny body, naked, walking over and retrieving the glass, but at the same time realized that he hadn't moved from the couch at all, and still wore his robe. He looked down and saw that the garment had opened, and despite the heat, modestly decided to cover himself. But he realized with some anxiety that he couldn't move his hands.

He looked at the TV, and saw the image of a boy a little older than he reclining on a plastic deck chair, bathed in the golden rays of the sun, wearing nothing but dark glasses. The camera, hand-held, slowly slithered toward him, and then moved in for a close-up of his face. His hair was slicked back, and his eyes disguised in those black wraparounds, but Miguelito gasped with recognition: it was his friend from the *zócalo,* Julio César.

The camera lovingly moved down Julio César's body, recording the contours of his narrow shoulders, the chest and torso, smooth except for a few sparse hairs above his uncircumcised penis, which he stroked absently. A close-up image of this fondling lingered for long moments, burning itself violently in Miguelito's brain.

The wide and strong hand of another man replaced Julio César's, and the frame expanded to include the sculpted torso of another figure, its strikingly golden blond bush and long, dangling purple penis submitting Miguelito to further shock. There was a cut to a medium shot of both figures. Miguelito identified the second man as Hunter who, in the frame, not without tenderness, grabbed a handful of Julio César's hair to angle the boy's face upward.

Miguelito's shock, based on shame and confusion, was overshadowed by some other feelings, including the warmth provided by the thick bathrobe. He couldn't quite put it together, but he realized that he had participated in some form of transaction, an illustration of Julio César's thesis that you can't get something for nothing. He owed something to Hunter, who had fed him lavishly, entertained him, and even saved his life in the swimming pool.

What he saw on TV seemed strange, scary, and disagreeable, but it was probably preferable to being on the street, at least if more of today's goodies were part of the bargain. His body felt as if it were sinking into the plump couch. With the same hand that touched Julio César in the film, Hunter began to stroke Miguelito's hair.

ACKNOWLEDGMENTS

Al que a buen árbol se arrima, buena sombra le cobija. I have been comforted by the shade offered me by the following people: Scott Baldinger, Bruce Benderson, Stuart Bernstein, Jennifer Carlson, Duncan Christy, Jacqueline Deval, Philip Herter, Robert Mc-Caskill, Daphne Merkin, Lucia Nevai, Shelley Perron, Don Shewey, Ann Treistman, and Jamie Wasserman. And I'm particularly grateful to my wife, Yehudit Mam, for never wavering, even when I did.